A Christmas for Chrissie

Love will OUT #5

D.E. Haggerty

Also By D.E. Haggerty

A Hero for Hailey
A Protector for Phoebe
A Fox for Faith
A Soldier for Suzie
A Valentine for Valerie
A Love for Lexi
My Forever Love
Forever For You
Just For Forever
Stay For Forever
Only Forever
Meet Disaster
Meet Not
Meet Dare
Meet Hate
Bragg's Truth
Bragg's Love
Perfect Bragg
About Face
At Arm's Length

Hands Off
Knee Deep
Molly's Misadventures

Chapter 1

Why is it called the Secret Service if everyone knows about it?

"WELCOME TO *YOU CHEAT, WE EAT,*" I greet the woman entering the PI offices. "How can I help you today?"

The woman pauses for a moment before screaming like a banshee and launching herself at me. I sigh before getting to my feet and rounding my desk to meet her. I barely stop myself from rolling my eyes at her. Does she seriously think she can take me on?

I'm five-foot-ten, highly trained, and keep myself in shape by lifting weights a few times a week and jogging nearly every day. The woman 'attacking' me is approximately five-foot-three, dressed in cumbersome clothing constraining her movements, and is obviously untrained.

I say untrained because she's flailing her arms at me like she's a windmill. Does she think she's Don Quixote? Snort. I *know* chivalry is dead unlike the knight errant who read way too many romances before deciding to revive the social code of conduct. Another reason to stay far, far away from romance.

I grasp her wrists and spin her around to pin them behind her back. The woman's shoulders slump and her legs give out from her as she wails. I maneuver her until she's sitting in a chair and release my hold on her.

"Hailey!" I shout because I can deal with danger, but I don't deal with emotion and a woman bawling her eyes out qualifies as emotion even if she did 'attack' me mere moments ago.

Hailey is my boss at *You Cheat, We Eat.* As the name suggests, the PI firm specializes in finding spouses who don't honor their vows. I'm nearly two decades older than my boss and I have the experience to work as a PI, but I'm not interested.

I'm done with wading through the filth of humanity, thank you very much. I'll stick to accounting, invoicing, filing, and the other boring administrative stuff for now. Although, I do run background checks for all the investigators.

Hailey rushes out of her office, a 9 mm in her hand. Her hand drops when she sees the woman sitting in the chair sobbing her heart out. "Oh."

I frown. "Yeah. Oh." I motion my hand toward the woman. "You're up."

Phoebe, the other PI at the firm, peeks her head out of her office. She blows out a breath of air when she realizes there's no danger. "I heard a scuffle, but the big guy wouldn't let me out of the room to back you up."

I raise an eyebrow and stare at her. Back me up? She's hilarious. One, I don't need backup. Ever. And two, Phoebe couldn't back me up if she tried. The woman is Ms. Fashionista. Seriously. She's currently wearing a dress that hugs all her curves and three-inch heels. I don't know anything about fashion, but I do know enough to recognize expensive, and her clothes are definitely expensive.

I hear a grunt before her husband, Ryker, joins her at the door. Ryker is a badass bounty hunter. At six-foot-six, he's a mountain of a man. I could still take him.

"Chrissie didn't need your help." He stares at me as if expecting me to respond to his statement with information about my background. He can keep staring because I'm not revealing any of my secrets to him or Hailey or Phoebe. I may consider the women my friends, but secrets are meant to remain private for a reason.

"It's all your fault," the woman screams and points at Hailey.

Hailey's eyes widen. "My fault? What did I do?"

"You caught my husband cheating and now he's left me for the other woman. He's not supposed to leave me for the other woman! He's supposed to fall to his knees and pledge his undying love to me."

I keep my face passive, but inside I'm shaking my head in disbelief at this woman. Someone else who's been reading too many romance novels.

Hailey's head tilts to the side as she studies the woman. "Mrs. Winter?" At the woman's nod, she kneels in front of her. "Why don't you come into my office, and we can discuss this?"

Mrs. Winter rears back. "What's there to discuss? Like you would know anything about betrayal with your perfect little life with your perfect little husband."

She's not wrong. Hailey married her high school crush, Aiden, at the beginning of the year. The two are still in their 'honeymoon' period and are disgustingly perfect. They can't keep their hands off of each other, but if they think they can have nookie time while I'm in charge of this office, they've got another thing coming.

Phoebe raises her hand. "I know a lot about betrayal. Do you want to get a coffee with me?"

Phoebe's not lying. I don't know the whole story, but her first husband apparently was a complete and utter dick. In fact, he's currently in prison for kidnapping her. He wanted to force her to have his children.

Gorgeous women always cause men to lose their minds and, make no mistake about it, Phoebe is gorgeous. She has exotic green eyes with a slight slant to them set in a heart-shaped face. And her body is a perfect hourglass shape.

Hailey is no slouch either. She doesn't have curves like Phoebe, but she has the whole lithe dancer body thing going on. With her long brown wavy hair and dark brown eyes, she looks like she was the head cheerleader in high school. She wasn't, though. Apparently, she was a bit of a drama geek and Aiden bullied her about it. There's definitely a story there.

Mrs. Winter glares at Phoebe. "What would you know about betrayal? You're beautiful."

And beautiful people don't know anything about betrayal? Trust me, betrayal is blind.

Ryker growls and stands in front of Phoebe. "You will not talk to my wife in this manner."

Sigh. He had to say wife, didn't he? Idiot. The word wife is totally going to set her off.

"Wife!" she screams and points at Phoebe. "You have no idea."

"You're done," Ryker declares before approaching Mrs. Winter. He hoists her from the chair by her arm before proceeding to escort her out of the office and down the hall to the elevator.

Once she's on the elevator with the doors closed behind her, he marches back to the office. He glares at me. "You should have handled her."

I raise an eyebrow. "She wasn't dangerous."

"She was rude to my wife."

"Rude doesn't equal dangerous. You should know this."

His nostrils flare as he stares at me. I fold my arms across my chest and stare right back at him. Does he think he can intimidate me? Silly man.

Phoebe tugs on her husband's arm. "Leave Chrissie alone. Her job isn't to keep me safe."

Before Ryker can speak, I do. "You weren't in danger, Phoebe. And I will make certain you're always safe when you're in the office."

"Maybe we should get you a weapon." Hailey's nose scrunches as she considers the idea. "This isn't the first crazy client we've had, and it won't be the last."

"I can deal with crazy." And I can. "Crazy doesn't equal dangerous, but I can deal with dangerous as well." Because I already have a weapon.

Ryker grunts and spins on his heel to return to his office. This is his M.O. whenever he thinks the talk will turn to 'women's shit'. His words. Not mine.

Phoebe and Hailey sit in the chairs across from my desk. They appear to be settling in for a talk. Oh goodie. In case you missed it, I'm being sarcastic.

"We can get the uncles to teach you to shoot," Hailey suggests.

The uncles aren't Hailey's blood relatives. It's a group of four men who served with Hailey's dad in the military.

"I don't need anyone to teach me how to shoot. Certainly not the uncles."

Phoebe waggles her eyebrows. "Not even Wally?"

At the mention of Wally, my belly flutters. The guy drives me absolutely bananas, but I can't deny he's one handsome man. I put his age somewhere in his fifties, but he doesn't look a day over forty.

His black hair doesn't have a hint of gray in it, although his beard is dotted with gray making him appear distinguished. Judging by his broad shoulders and strong biceps, he keeps himself in shape. And I do appreciate a man who takes care of himself. But it's his eyes that get to me. They're dark green and when he stares at me, it's like he's peering into my soul.

Wally and the rest of the 'uncles' retired from the Army ages ago, but I suspect Wally hasn't completely retired, however. Not when I know he's been digging into my past. He's pissed off because he ran into a brick wall. A brick wall I have no intention of pulling down or letting him scale. Skeletons should stay hidden in the closet for a reason.

"I can shoot."

Hailey leans closer. "You can? How did you learn? When did you learn? Where did you learn?"

I don't fill her in on the details. They don't need to know the US government taught me to shoot nearly every weapon known to man. I shrug instead.

"It doesn't matter."

Phoebe giggles. "Wrong thing to say. Now, you've made her curious. She's going to dig and dig until she finds out all the answers to her questions."

Hailey frowns. "I think you have me confused with Suzie. I can allow my friends to have secrets."

Suzie is Hailey's business partner. She used to be the office manager until her brewery business took off. Now, she spends her days brewing beer and I do her job.

Phoebe snorts. "Yeah, right."

The phone rings and offers me a reprieve. I know better than to dive on the distraction, though. Diving would pique Hailey's curiosity more than it already is. She won't find anything if she digs around in my past, but I don't want to spend the rest of my working days evading her questions either.

"Are you going to answer the phone?" Hailey asks.

"Are we finished with this conversation? I didn't want to appear rude."

Hailey stands. "We're done."

Phoebe's nose wrinkles. "We are?"

As I watch Hailey and Phoebe return to their respective offices, I think about how exhausting it is to be friends with people you can't tell the truth about your past. This is why I've never had close friends outside people I met at 'the office' before. I should back off from their friendship for a while. I nod to myself. It's for the best.

Decision made, I pick up the phone.

Chapter 2

If you think your computer, laptop, and phone spying on you is scary then think again, because your vacuum cleaner has been gathering dirt on you for years.

DESPITE PROMISING TO DISTANCE myself from Hailey, Phoebe, and their group of friends, I find myself in the parking lot of McGraw's Pub a few hours later. McGraw's is a bar owned by Hailey's dad, Max, who everyone calls Pops. It's also where Hailey's uncles hang out as if the place is their own personal living room.

Hailey insisted we meet here tonight as her dad and his brand-spanking-new fiancée, Faith, returned from a weekend in Cancun this morning. It was a surprise trip Pops sprung on Faith the day after the two got engaged on Thanksgiving. Hailey wants to check in with Faith to see how she's handling everything.

As I walk toward the entrance, I feel someone's eyes on me and slow my pace. I canvas the area and sure enough, Wally is standing underneath a streetlight with his gaze aimed at me. I stop and wait. He obviously has something to say, and I prefer he says it out here where no one else can overhear. This group of friends is all up in each other's business. They won't hesitate to eavesdrop on our conversation if we're inside the bar.

I tap my foot as I wait for Wally to cross the parking lot. "What is it this time?"

"Who are you?" he asks.

"Christina Lindberg, aka Chrissie."

"Don't be a smartass. You know what I mean."

He means he did a background check on me and ran into a big, fat blackhole. Why he thinks I'm going to fill him in is beyond me. We're not friends. More like frenemies. Besides, I won't be filling in my friends about my past either.

I shrug and twirl around to open the door to the pub. Wally grabs my upper arm to stop me. I don't think so. I jerk out of his hold and whirl around at him with my fists at the ready. He retreats with his hands raised.

"I mean you no harm."

I snort and drop my hands. "Then, stop sticking your nose where it doesn't belong."

His nostrils flare before he strides forward right into my personal space. "You are my business."

Before I have a chance to respond, Suzie shouts, "Kiss her!"

I glance to my side to find Suzie and her husband Grayson have arrived. Suzie is bouncing on her toes while clapping her hands. "Kiss her!" she shouts again.

Suzie is tiny at just two inches over five feet, but what she lacks in height, she makes up for in personality. The woman is a troublemaking firecracker. Appropriate since her hair is fire engine red. She's also a complete klutz.

Her husband wraps an arm around her and pulls her close. "Calm down, munchkin. You can't be bouncing around when you're pregnant."

She rolls her eyes at him. "Chill, dude. I want six kids. Six children equals a whole lot of pregnant time. Get used to it."

Six kids? Is the woman crazy? I watch for Grayson's reaction. He obviously doesn't think she's crazy. His eyes warm as he stares down at her. He waggles his eyebrows. "It's also a whole lot of practicing."

"Yeah!" Suzie shouts and throws her arms in the air.

Time for me to make my exit while everyone is preoccupied with the crazy girl. I grip the door handle, but before I can open the door, Wally whispers in my ear, "This isn't over."

Goosebumps break out over my skin at the feel of his warm breath on my skin. I manage to contain my shiver. Thank goodness. I can't give the man any ammunition to use against me. He's a pain in my ass as it is.

The bar is nearly empty when I enter. The uncles are sitting at their booth in the corner and a few barflies are bellied up to the bar.

As soon as Wally strolls in behind me, Lenny grins. "Pay up! I told you he wouldn't get any information from her."

Barney and Sid, the other two uncles, groan before slapping money on the table.

"Thanks, doll." Lenny winks at me.

I ignore him. I'm not evading Wally's questions to fill Lenny's pockets. I scan the area and notice Hailey and Phoebe in a back booth with their men. As soon as they notice me, Hailey waves me over before shoving her husband out of the booth.

"Go. We have girl stuff to talk about."

Aiden and Ryker practically run away when they hear 'girl stuff'.

"Where's Faith?" I ask when I sit down.

"She'll be down in a minute," Pops says. He sets a beer down in front of me before leaving to return to the bar.

Suzie picks up my beer. She sniffs it before setting it back down. "This is cruel and unusual punishment. I have to watch everyone drink, but I can't drink myself."

"It's worth it, trust me," Faith says as she joins us.

Faith is a few years younger than me. She ended up in Milwaukee because her son landed in some trouble back in Saint Louis. Pops stepped in to help her out and they fell in love. It's not hard to figure out why Pops went all out to help her. Besides being sweet as apple pie, she's pretty and when she smiles – something she's doing a lot of lately – she transforms from pretty to beautiful.

Hailey rubs her hands together. "Someone had a good time in Cancun. Tell us all about it."

Suzie claps. "Yes! All the deets, please."

Phoebe groans. "No. Please don't. I don't want to hear about Pops having sex."

"Oh, come on." Suzie bumps her shoulder. "Pops is a stone-cold fox." She waggles her eyebrows. "You know he's got skills."

Pops is what the romance novels call a silver fox. His hair may be silver, but the man doesn't look a day over forty despite being in his mid-fifties. He's tall with broad shoulders and a narrow waist. He obviously takes good care of himself. And he has these bright, blue eyes you want to dive right into.

Faith giggles and her eyes stray to her fiancé who – surprise, surprise! – can't keep his eyes off of her. I wouldn't be shocked if the evening is cut short because they want to escape and have some alone time. Although, Faith's son, Ollie, is probably upstairs.

"I'm not talking about sex with my fiancé with his daughter in attendance."

Suzie points to Hailey. "You! Go!"

Hailey grunts. She's not going anywhere.

Suzie frowns. "If we can't hear about Faith and Pops getting it on, I want to hear why Wally had Chrissie pinned to the front door when we arrived."

All heads swivel in my direction. I narrow my eyes and stare at Suzie. I count to ten before she starts to fidget. Got her! She grunts. "Fine! I retract my query."

"Nuh-uh." Hailey shakes her head. "Now, I'm curious."

Before I can level my stare on Hailey, Pops arrives. He sets a glass of wine in front of Faith and leans down to kiss her. This is not some quick kiss. No, he sips on her lips.

Phoebe gags and covers her eyes with her hands. "Someone tell me when they're finished."

"They're finished," Suzie immediately says.

Phoebe drops her hand to discover Pops now has his hand around Faith's neck and they're practically making out. She shoves Suzie. "You're cruel!"

Suzie rubs her hands together. "Mwa ha ha."

Barney shouts from across the room. "Why was the guitar teacher arrested?"

Barney is the jokester of the uncles. As far as I can tell, he only tells dirty jokes. And mostly they're corny, dirty jokes. He finds himself hilarious.

Pops ends the kiss and glares over his shoulder at Barney. "I told you no more dirty jokes in Faith's presence."

"Dude," Barney scoffs. "I'm pretty confident Faith knows what sex is by now. Otherwise, we need to schedule a doctor's appointment for your blue balls after a weekend in Cancun of not getting laid."

Pops stands to his full height, but before he can advance in Barney's direction, Faith grasps his hand to stop him. "Let him be. He's trying to rile you up on purpose and you're playing right into his hands."

Barney sighs. "Dang. Faith is going to steal all my fun away."

"I can help you have some fun." His head swivels to the entry of the pub where Valerie stands. She winks at him. "Naked fun. Hint. Hint. Nudge. Nudge."

Valerie is a friend of Faith's from Saint Louis. She showed up last week at Thanksgiving dinner and practically jumped Barney the moment she saw him.

Sid slaps a bill down on the table. "I'm going broke here. How is it Barney hasn't jumped on the offer she's obviously making?"

Wally collects the money from Sid and Lenny. "Because he's a scaredy-cat."

Sid frowns at Barney. "Dude, it's like riding a bike. Just get on and ride."

Valerie giggles. "I love this place," she says as she joins our table.

"I thought you'd be back in Saint Louis by now," Hailey says.

"She's staying in my apartment for a while. I couldn't get out of the lease until the first of the year anyway. Someone might as well enjoy it," Faith answers.

"Which is why Barney is avoiding me. He's afraid I'll 'catch feelings'." Valerie snorts. "As if."

I tilt my head as I study the woman. I'd guess she's about Faith's age of forty-five. She's also around Faith's height, which is several inches shorter than me. But unlike Faith, she's not some skinny woman. No, she's voluptuous with curves in all the right places. Some would call her fat, but she wears her extra weight with confidence.

"What is going on with the uncles? They've never been loved up before, but now Sid's married, Wally's chasing after Chrissie, and Barney is allowing Valerie to chase after him." Suzie squints at the uncles as if she doesn't recognize them anymore.

Valerie leans toward me. "Wally's chasing you?" She glances over at the uncles' table and licks her lips. "I wouldn't make him chase me much."

"Who's ready to get their asses kicked in pool?" I ask because I'm not talking about Wally and me. There's nothing to talk about. The butterflies in my stomach call me a liar, but I ignore them. I'm an expert in ignoring my body's needs.

Chapter 3

I've been interrogating the dog for two hours. He still won't tell me who's a good boy.

WALLY

I slam the beer down on the bar with a grunt.

"Someone got up on the wrong side of the bed this morning," Lenny says, and I snarl at him. He raises his hands in surrender. "Don't take your sexual frustration out on me, man." He pauses. "Unless you want to, of course." He waggles his eyebrows.

Lenny would probably be up for it. He is bisexual after all. Personally, I couldn't care less which side he butters his bread on, but I have no interest in shaking boots with the man.

"Pass."

He shrugs. "What's got your panties in a twist then?"

Max chuckles. "I think you mean who not what. Her name starts with a C and ends with -rissie."

Sid slaps a hand on my shoulder. "Why haven't you taken the blonde for a test drive yet?"

I growl. "Don't talk about her like she's some floozy."

"Pay up fucker," Sid says and holds his hand out to Max.

Max holds up his hands. "I didn't bet with you."

"Of course, you did. You said Wally wasn't interested in Chrissie," Sid insists.

Max chuckles. "Like hell I did. I'm not blind. Hell, even a blind man can see he's obsessed with the woman."

"I am not obsessed with anyone," I grit out.

I'm lying. I can't stop thinking about the woman. I want to pull on her blonde ponytail while I stare into her light blue eyes before molding my lips to hers. My other hand will be busy exploring her curves. The woman is in great shape. She obviously works to stay in condition, but she has curves I can't wait to get my hands on.

The door to McGraw's bangs open as Barney saunters in whistling. He smirks at our group. "What's the difference between a tire and 365 used condoms?"

I swallow my groan. I'm not in the mood for Barney's corny sex jokes, but I can't show my irritation. The guys have obviously cottoned on to my obsession with Chrissie. I know better than to hand them any further ammunition.

"One's a Goodyear. The other's a *great* year." Barney guffaws at his own joke. He holds up his hand to bump my fist, but I ignore him. He doesn't need any encouragement.

When no one bumps his fist, he drops his hand. "What's going on?"

"Nothing," I say at the same time as Max says, "Wally's down in the dumps because Chrissie won't give him the time of day."

I'm not worried about Chrissie giving me the time of day. I saw the goosebumps rise on her skin when I whispered in her ear. I know she's affected by me. If I press her, I could get her in my bed. But I don't want her in my bed. At least, I don't want her *only* in my bed. I want to get to know the mysterious woman. But I can't get to know her unless I know she's not dangerous. Her background check tells me she's most definitely dangerous.

Damn. I'm going to have to come clean with my brothers. They'll just needle me until I tell them anyway.

"I ran Chrissie."

Max snorts. "Of course, you did."

"What did you find out?" Sid asks.

"Something bad obviously. Thus, the rotten mood," Lenny says.

Barney rubs his hands together while smiling like a loon. "What did you find? Does she have a record? Is she a car jacker? Or maybe a jewelry thief?"

I frown. "She doesn't have a record."

Barney scratches his beard. "I'm confused. Is anyone else confused?"

Max throws his rag down and leans on his elbows on the bar. "She's clean? I figured you found out something sinister and have been sitting on the information because you're interested in her."

He's not exactly wrong. "Her background came back clean. Too clean. Squeaky clean."

Max cocks an eyebrow. "You think she's hiding something."

"Is she in danger?" Lenny asks.

"Good." Sid nods. "Things were getting a bit boring around here."

I raise an eyebrow. "A bit boring. We went down to Saint Louis to deal with Faith's problems last month."

"And we saw zero action," Sid complains.

"I wouldn't call loading up a gang hang-out with drugs and guns while the gang members slept in the same house zero action," I point out.

"But no one woke up. We didn't get into any fights. Hell, I didn't draw my weapon once. Boring." Sid draws out the word like he's a teenager and not the fifty-something man I know he is.

"I have a feeling whatever's going on with Chrissie isn't boring."

Lenny raises an eyebrow. "Why? What did you discover?"

I frown. "Nothing. Gut feeling."

My brothers know not to question my gut. It's saved our asses more times than I can count.

"Why don't you use your fancy connections to dig into Chrissie further?" Max asks.

Hailey and Suzie aren't wrong when they call me a super-secret spy, although I prefer the term operative myself. The guys retired once we finished our twenty-year stint in the army. I never actually retired. I can't sit around and play poker all day long every day. I need the action. And, as long as I have skills our government can use, I'll keep working to make the world a safe place for Americans to live and travel in.

"I've tried."

Max's eyes widen at my response. Exactly. I should be able to dig into the background of every single person in the entire world. But with Chrissie, I'm coming up against a brick wall.

"Do you think she's in WITSEC?" Lenny asks.

Witness protection was my first guess. The US Marshalls never reveal the names of those under their protection, not even to me. But knowing what I do of the types of cases that warrant their protection, I did some research. I searched cases around the time Chrissie showed up in our lives and came up with a big fat nothing. I give it less than a three percent chance she's in WITSEC.

"Doesn't fit."

"Crap. You think we got ourselves a Phoebe situation?" Barney asks.

Phoebe was hiding from her ex-husband when she landed in Milwaukee and took a job at Hailey and Suzie's PI firm. Everyone could tell Phoebe was scared when she arrived. We knew she was hiding something but until she trusted me with her last name, we were powerless to help her.

"No way. Chrissie wouldn't hide from anyone."

The woman who's gone toe to toe with me twice would never run away from her problems. She's not the type to back down from a threat. She's the type to head straight into danger.

"You sound like you admire her," Sid points out. "I predict another wedding in our future."

"Just because you've been married six times and counting doesn't mean the rest of us want to get married."

Sid slaps my shoulder and the force of it nearly has me bending forward. "None of this 'and counting'. Mary Ann has made an honest man of me."

I believe him. He's different with Mary Ann than he was with his previous wives. Except for his first wife, of course. The one he put on a pedestal who deserted him while he was away protecting our country. There's only one word to describe her – bitch. But Sid still won't hear a negative word about her.

"Speak for yourself," Max says. "I can't wait to get married again."

Max got burned by his first wife, too, but she didn't leave him. No, Max kicked her ass out when she refused to be a good mother to Hailey. It took him twelve years, but at least he didn't put up with her shit forever.

The minute Faith walked into the door and Max saw her, he fell. He took his time courting her, though, which was exactly what Faith needed. He proposed to her last week at Thanksgiving and the man hasn't stopped smiling since. I'm happy for him but I'm also a bit envious.

Barney scowls. "Marriage isn't for me." I can't blame him after what happened to him.

"Enough of this marriage talk," Lenny insists. The man doesn't believe in marriage since he can't stick to either a male or female partner. He needs both, but he's yet to meet a woman or man who can handle what he needs. "What are you going to do about Chrissie?"

"Maybe you should leave it alone. If she's not in danger, let her have her secrets," Max says.

"I can't confirm she's not in danger, and I'm one-hundred percent positive something's off."

"In that case, brother, you're going to have to go old school."

I nod at his suggestion. I already knew this, of course. But I wanted someone else to make the suggestion. It makes invading Chrissie's privacy less of an ethical violation. Most people believe my 'job' has robbed me of an ethical meter. They're wrong.

Barney claps his hands. "Since we've got all of Wally's problems settled, who's up for a game of pool?"

My problems aren't settled. Not in the least. But I don't say anything because they will be settled. I'll figure out what's going on with Chrissie and solve her problems. She'll thank me eventually. Probably.

Chapter 4

What similarities do peeping toms and spies share? They both see things they shouldn't.

"Incoming!" I shout to Hailey when Pops wanders into *You Cheat, We Eat* on Thursday morning.

Ryker and Phoebe aren't in the office today. Phoebe is working an insurance case, and Ryker is playing Mr. Protector as in following her every step to ensure she doesn't break a nail. It's utterly ridiculous, but it's also kind of adorable how much he cares for his wife.

Pops grins and saunters to my desk. "How you doing, darling?"

I bristle at his use of the word darling. I'm not his darling. But then I remember he's not my boss trying to use my gender against me and force a smile on my face.

"All right. What are you doing here?"

It's not like Hailey's dad to drop by. Actually, I've only worked at the PI firm for a little over a month. Maybe he does drop by on the odd occasion.

"Hey, Pops." Hailey hugs her dad. "What's up?"

"Maybe I wanted to check out where my baby girl works."

She rolls her eyes. "What do you need?"

Pops chuckles before sobering and admitting, "I need you to find someone for me."

Her eyes widen. "Me? Why don't you use your contacts?"

Pops has contacts? Interesting. I know him and the uncles are former Army. I assumed, based on a few things they've said here and there, they're former special forces. No need to assume any longer. Regular Army don't have the contacts needed to find someone.

He shrugs and Hailey giggles. "You came up with nothing, didn't you?"

Now, I'm intrigued. Who does he need to find who's hiding from him?

When Pops says nothing, Hailey asks, "Who are you searching for?"

"Silas Bakman."

Bakman? Faith's last name is Bakker, except Bakker isn't actually her last name. She changed it when she fled Saint Louis for Milwaukee. Bakman, Bakker. Pretty much the same name. And Silas is her ex-husband's name.

"You're trying to find Ollie's biological father," I guess.

At Pops' nods, Hailey squeals. "Yes! I'm getting a little brother. Finally!"

Faith's son, Oliver, is hardly little. He's fifteen and nearly as tall as Hailey, who at five-foot-eight is no slouch.

"In order to adopt Ollie, we need to notify his biological father of the petition to adopt."

"Doesn't Faith know where he is? After all, he's paying child support, isn't he?"

At Hailey's question, Pops grumbles, "The dick hasn't paid child support since Ollie was ten years old."

I'm not surprised. From what Faith's said, Ollie's dad is a total jerk who didn't help pay the bills when they were still married.

"What do we know about Silas the dick?" Hailey asks, and I grab a pen and paper to take notes.

"Not much," Pops begins and then gives me his last known address, the address of his parents, and his last known place of work.

"I'll get right on it," I tell him when he finishes.

"Thanks, darling." This time I don't bristle when he uses the term.

As soon as Pops leaves, Hailey sighs. "If Pops couldn't find Ollie's dad, I don't think we can either."

She has no clue of the resources I have. I have no plans of telling her about my past, though. "I'll give it a go."

"Thanks, Chrissie."

I don't respond. I'm already bringing up the programs to search for Silas.

I need two hours, which is ninety minutes longer than I thought, to find the man. Silas went completely off-grid two years ago. He got off all social media, closed his banking accounts, removed his information from data mining sites, and disappeared. There are usually two reasons for a person to go off-grid – he's a doomsday prepper or he committed a crime and is hiding.

I don't know enough about Silas to make a judgment on his reasons for going off-grid and, frankly, I don't care. My sole mission is to find the man. I finally hit pay dirt when I checked the phone records for Mr. and Mrs. Oscar Bakman in Saint Louis. Silas doesn't call his parents often, but he called them three months ago from a pay phone in Idaho. After that, it was a simple matter of searching the local trailer parks before I found a man meeting Silas' description.

I knock on Hailey's door before sticking my head inside. "I found him."

Her mouth gapes open. "You did? I thought we'd have to call Wally for help since Pops couldn't find him."

I snort. Like Wally has better connections than mine. "Do you want me to call Pops?"

She glances at the clock on the wall. "Why don't you head over to McGraw's instead? You can pick us up some lunch while you're there."

My stomach warms at the idea. It's because the food at the pub is good, not because Wally might be there. Fine. Maybe my stomach is tingling a teensy bit in anticipation of meeting Wally. The man is one fine specimen of manhood. Too bad he's a dick.

When I stroll into McGraw's Pub fifteen minutes later, the place is packed. Pops waves me over to the bar.

"Hailey called in your to-go order. It should be ready in a few minutes. You want a drink while you wait?"

Instead of answering his question, I state, "I have some information for you."

He freezes. "You do? This quickly?"

I remove the slip of paper with Silas' current address from my pocket and slide it across the bar. "Here you go."

He places his hand on the paper, but he doesn't pick it up. He's too busy staring at me.

"What's going on?" Wally asks from behind me.

I don't startle. I knew he was coming up behind me. Situational awareness is Day 1 learning material.

"Nothing. Pops needed some help."

I'm not being cagey on purpose. I'm protective of Pops' privacy is all. Maybe Pops wants to tell Faith he found Silas before he tells his brothers.

"Nothing?" Pops cocks an eyebrow. "You being a miracle worker isn't nothing."

A miracle worker? Not hardly. Using governmental resources I shouldn't have access to any longer is not performing miracles.

Wally places his hand on my lower back, and I swear I feel a current of electricity zap me. I have to swallow the gasp the feeling of him touching me causes. This man affects my body like no man before him.

He whispers into my ear. "What did you do?"

There's a bite to his words as if he thinks I've been up to no good. What is wrong with this man? Why is he such a dick to me? I swear I didn't do anything to him.

I step out of his reach and whirl around to confront him. "What the hell is your problem?"

"Chrissie, Wally," Pops scolds. "Try not to kill each other during my lunch hour rush please."

"Tell me what you did, and I'll let it go," Wally demands.

I roll my eyes. Demanding an answer is not the way to go.

Pops comes around the bar to stand in between us. He glares at Wally. "Brother, you need to calm down. She did me a favor." He grins at me. "A favor for which I'm extremely grateful."

Wally growls, and Pops winks at me. Is Pops deliberately egging Wally on? Men! I'll never understand them. Not if I live to be a million years old.

I'm done with this stupid conversation. "Is our food ready?"

"I'll check. Why don't you tell Wally what the favor was in the meantime?"

I raise an eyebrow. "You don't want to tell Faith first?"

He doesn't answer as he saunters away.

"Well?"

Wally stands with his arms crossed over his chest. The action makes his biceps pop. I don't care if the man is nearly sixty years old. He's got arm candy for days.

"What's the favor you did for Pops?"

At his question, I tear my gaze away from his arms to find him smirking at me. Jerk. He couldn't pretend to not notice my obsession with his arms?

"I found Silas," I don't hesitate to tell him since Pops okayed it.

Wally stills. "Silas as in Faith's ex?" I nod. "Pops told me he couldn't find him."

Duh. He wouldn't have asked someone else to try to find Silas if he already had. "Which is why he asked Hailey to look into it."

"Hailey found him?"

I shake my head. "No, I did." He doesn't appear convinced. "It's not like it was hard." It was a little hard. "Silas went off-grid two years ago, but no one can go completely off-grid."

"How'd you find him?"

"He called his parents from a payphone in Idaho."

His eyes narrow. "You have access to phone records?"

I'm not going to dignify his question with a response. He knows I shouldn't have access to phone records.

"Who are you, Christina Lindberg?"

I wiggle my eyebrows. "Do you need my social security number yet?"

As if it would help him. Besides, we both know he's got the number already.

Pops interrupts our stare down to hand me my food. "How much do I owe you?"

"Darling, your money is no good here."

"Thank you. Have a good day."

I wave as I strut off. I don't look back. I don't need to. I know Wally is watching every step I take – it's the reason I'm strutting after all – since I can feel his eyes burning a hole in my back.

Chapter 5

My neighbor thinks I spy on her. I would tell her otherwise, but she's in the shower right now.

WALLY

I stare at Chrissie's house from where I'm sitting in my truck parked down the street. When Pops told me to go old school, this is what he meant. Good old-fashioned surveillance. Unfortunately, there hasn't been much to surveil this week.

I realize it's early days. It's only the third night I've sat outside Chrissie's house, and this type of work can take weeks if not months. I don't have months. Trouble is brewing around Chrissie. I'd bet my security clearance on it. And I need to know what. Otherwise, I can't protect her.

I study the house. It's nothing like what I expected the woman Chrissie to own. I imagined a sleek, modern house not dissimilar to my own. But Chrissie's house is a cute cottage. It's painted light blue with white trim. The front porch runs the length of the house and has a porch swing on it. There's even a white fence around her yard.

A light is on in the living room revealing Chrissie moving around. She came home at the exact same time she came home on the previous two days. If someone is after her, she's making it easy for them. She needs to vary her schedule to make her location unpredictable.

Another half-hour passes before all the lights are switched off and Chrissie settles in for the night. Time to make my move. I don't know what I can find roaming around the perimeter of Chrissie's house, but I'm too impatient to spend the next however many weeks following her.

Especially after learning she has access to phone records today. Accessing phone records is beyond Hailey's PI capabilities. You need a warrant for access unless you work for certain governmental organizations. I've checked with those governmental organizations. Christina Lindberg's name did not come up.

I exit my car making certain to not make a sound when I shut the door. The neighbor's yard doesn't have a fence, so I traipse through the shadows of the backyard until I reach Chrissie's fence. I leap over it and then pause to make sure there's no movement from Chrissie's house. Not a curtain is stirring. I hunch down and creep toward the sliding door off her back deck.

I'm on the first stair when I hear it. The unmistakable sound of the slide moving forward to chamber a round in a handgun. A second later I feel the cool metal against my temple.

"I thought you were better than this," Chrissie says.

I raise my arms. "I am." Except I'm standing in her backyard with a gun against my head. How did this happen? I underestimated Chrissie is what happened.

"Why are you here?"

"Why don't we talk inside where your neighbors can't observe us?" I tilt my head to the side where a light in the neighbor's house just went on.

"Fine," she huffs. "But we will discuss your trespassing."

"Of course," I readily agree.

The pressure of the gun against my temple disappears and I whirl around to confront Chrissie, but she's already gone. The woman has skills, but they can't be skills our government taught her. I would have found out otherwise.

The sliding door opens and Chrissie motions me inside. The door opens into the kitchen. The kitchen matches the outside of the house with its light blue Shaker cabinets with gray penny tiles for a backsplash. The floor is a light pine wood.

"Sit." Chrissie points to the kitchen table.

"How did you get the drop on me?" I ask as soon as I'm sitting.

She purses her lips as she sits across from me. "Why were you sneaking around my yard?"

I rub a hand down my face. "I'm not stalking you."

She snorts. "Following me from the office to the gym to home and then sitting outside in your truck all night is the very definition of stalking."

"You made me?"

She rolls her eyes.

"Why didn't you say something?"

"I was waiting for you to make your move. I figured you'd have more patience, though. Three days? Really?" She sounds unimpressed. As she should be. No wonder she got the drop on me, she made me three days ago.

I shrug. "I have a bad feeling."

She sighs. "Men and their gut feelings."

"Women have intuition. Why can't men have gut feelings?"

"The only thing women's intuition will get you is in a boatload of trouble."

I sit up. "Are you in a boatload of trouble?"

She grimaces. She obviously didn't want to give me any information. "Not anymore."

I reach across the table to grasp her hand. I'm surprised she doesn't jerk away. "How can you be certain?" I ask as I squeeze her hand.

Now, she does jerk her hand away. "Trust me. I know."

She stands. "I think it's time for you to leave. You can go through the front door."

She indicates the door with a sweep of her hand. My eyes scan the room. The kitchen is open to the living room. The living room looks as comfortable as I suspected. An L-shaped couch occupies most of the space. Across from it is an entertainment center with a television big enough to watch football on. The blue and gray theme continues in there, but there are also multi-colored pillows and rugs to add color.

But there's one thing missing – Christmas decorations. Almost everyone has decorated for the holiday already since Thanksgiving was last week.

"Where are your Christmas decorations?"

Pain flashes over her face before her mask comes down. "I don't do Christmas anymore."

The word anymore is spoken softly, almost too softly to hear, but I do hear. "Why not anymore?"

Her eyes narrow on me. "This is not up for discussion."

My legs move before I can stop them. It's not as if I want to stop them. I can't stand the pain clear to read on Chrissie's face. If I had it my way, she'd never experience a moment of pain in her life again. I cup her face with my hands.

"Angel," I begin and Chrissie snarls.

"I'm not your angel. I'm not your anything."

I caress her face. "You could be."

She leans back forcing me to drop my hands. "You could give a woman whiplash. One minute you're accusing me of bringing trouble to your friends. The next minute you're acting like you want me."

I crowd her, but she doesn't retreat. On no, not my Chrissie. She holds her ground. "I'm not acting. I do want you."

"Then, let this quest to find out every single thing about me go."

I wish I could give her this. I'd give her nearly anything she wants, but in this, I can't give in. "I can't."

"Why can't you?" She snarls. "I give you my word I'm not a danger to your crew."

Fuck. I need to let this go. She'll never learn to trust me if I don't accept her word. I try for a compromise. "Give me something. Make it real."

She studies my face for a long time. I listen to the sound of the kitchen clock tick, while I keep my gaze focused on her. After several minutes pass, she nods.

"I don't like Christmas because my parents died on Christmas day. It was a car accident. They were on their way to visit me. The rest of my family blames me for my parents' death. They shouldn't have been driving with the weather conditions the way they were, but they didn't want me to spend Christmas alone."

"And now you spend every Christmas alone."

She doesn't respond. She doesn't need to. Her answer is plain to read on her face and in the lack of decorations around her house.

"Not this year, you won't," I declare before wrapping my arms around her. There's a moment of hesitation before she returns my hug. I sway her from side to side and she clings to my back. "You'll come to McGraw's Pub."

She leans back to study my face. "You have Christmas at the bar? What about your own family?"

"Angel, those men are my brothers. They are my family."

She nods. "I understand." She bites her lip. I know what she wants to ask, and I have no problems telling her.

"I don't have any family in the area. I've got a brother in California. I visit him and his family a few times a year."

"When you're out west for work?"

I chuckle. "Now you're digging."

"Like you haven't been digging about me."

"I can't tell you about my work."

"I understand," she says without hesitation.

I squeeze her one more time before releasing her. "You'll come to McGraw's for Christmas then?"

She cocks her head. "You'll stop digging into my background?"

Damn. I did promise to stop digging around if she gave me something real, and there's not much more real than your parents dying. "I will."

She smiles, but I raise my hand before she can celebrate her victory.

"I'm not finished. If trouble comes around, I'm not holding back."

She holds out her hand. "Deal."

We shake on it. "It's late. Time for me to head home." I don't want to. Having Chrissie in my arms is right where I want her to be, but I know she needs time. I won't give her much time, but I'll give her the illusion of time at least.

"Lock up after me," I order as I open the front door.

"Yeah, yeah, Mr. Bossy."

Despite knowing I don't need to, I stand on the porch and wait for the sound of the lock engaging before leaving. When I hear the beep of the alarm being set, I grin. There's my girl!

Chapter 6

Why did the spy cross the road? He didn't. He was never on your side.

I square my shoulders before I open the door to McGraw's Pub the next night. I'm not afraid. Seriously, I'm not. But I am weirded out by the way Wally is acting. I know we have chemistry – the air practically cackles when we're near – but I'm not ready for him to call me angel. In fact, I don't think I'll be ready for another relationship ever again. Not after how the last one went up in flames. I'm being literal. There were actual flames shooting into the air.

I nearly turn around and walk my behind right out of the place when the noise level of the bar hits me. It's Friday night. I expected the place to be busy, but this is ridiculous. It's standing room only. What the hell is going on? The Friday the week after Thanksgiving isn't some holiday I don't know about, is it?

"Can you believe this?" Hailey has to shout her question to be heard over the noise.

"What's going on?"

"Apparently I'm now a famous YouTuber." She beams as she surveys the bar.

"What?"

Has she been secretly uploading videos on YouTube? I'm surprised Aiden would allow her. Her detective husband is nearly as protective of her as Ryker is of Phoebe. Why is anyone's guess. Hailey can handle herself, and she's not afraid to tell anyone who tries to push her around what she thinks of them.

"The video from Pops' proposal to Faith on Thanksgiving went viral."

I study the room and note the vast majority of the patrons are women. Plenty of women visit the pub, but they're usually with their partners. McGraw's Pub doesn't exactly scream girl's night out. And these women aren't dressed for a night at a bar, not with their skintight dresses and puffed-up hair. Nope, these women are on the prowl.

I gaze down at my own outfit. I'm wearing a thick sweater and jeans with a pair of sturdy, leather boots. It's cold out and the smell of the first snowfall is in the air. There's no way I'm leaving the house in some skimpy dress. Don't get me wrong. I don't hate the cold. I'll choose cold over hot ass desert any day of the year, but I also know better than to expose my naked legs to the freezing cold.

I lean close to Hailey, so I don't have to shout. "I don't get it. Pops is engaged. Why are they all dressed like maneaters?"

She points to the uncles' table. "They're why. According to the comments on the video, there's more than one silver fox at McGraw's Pub."

"Ridiculous. None of them have gray hair." Wally has a bit of gray in his beard, but it doesn't qualify him as a silver fox. Although, he is a fox.

As I watch, a group of women converge on the table. One woman sits down right in Sid's lap. He picks her up and removes her from his lap before waving his wedding band in her face. Lenny winks at her before motioning for her to join him. Another woman occupies the spot next to Wally.

My feet are moving before I tell them to. Wally smiles when he notices me. He presses on the woman's shoulder until she gets the hint and stands. He scoots out of the booth and saunters to me. When he reaches me, he wraps an arm around me before kissing my forehead. "I'm happy you're here, Angel."

I raise an eyebrow. "Are you seriously afraid of a bunch of women, Wally?"

"He calls her angel!" Suzie shouts up at me.

"Where did you come from?" I didn't notice her when I scanned the room and I notice everything.

"The restroom. Morning sickness is bull cocky. It should be called all day and night sickness."

Grayson sighs. "Which is why you should be at home resting."

I feel Wally's body shake with the laughter he's trying to contain. He knows as well as I do how much trouble Grayson jumped into.

Suzie's hands fist on her hips making her baby bump protrude. "I should stay at home and rest because I'm pregnant! What century are we living in, huh?"

She pokes his chest, and he grabs her hand and pulls her near. He bends over to whisper into her ear. I don't know what he's saying, but it must be good because she practically melts into him.

When he stands back up, she grabs his hand before announcing, "We're leaving. We have things to do. Sexy things to do." She waggles her eyebrows before dragging Grayson out of the place. Although, I guess it's not really dragging since he's smiling wide, and his eyes are zeroed in on Suzie's ass.

Sid joins us. "I sink I'll leaf," he slurs.

"Dude, do you need me to order you a taxi?" I ask the obviously inebriated man.

"Thot drunk." Yeah, sure he isn't. There's actual drool dripping down his chin.

Barney slaps his back. "He's not drunk. His mouth is numb."

I shiver. I hate the dentist. "Dental work?"

"I suspect someone had numbing gel in his toothpaste today," Barney answers.

My nose wrinkles. "Why would you put numbing gel in your toothpaste?"

Sid glares at Wally. "I thidn't."

I glance up at the man whose arm is still wrapped around me. Darn it. Why is it this comfortable being in his arms? I should probably move, but it's like Wally can read my thoughts. He tightens his arm around me and whispers into my ear, "You're not going anywhere."

"What did you do to Sid?" I ask instead of dealing with feelings and icky stuff.

"It's not a big deal. No one's going to get hurt from a bit of numbing gel."

Sid shoves Wally's shoulder. "Mary Ann."

"Like I didn't notice two different tubes of toothpaste on your vanity."

My eyes widen. "Did you seriously break into Sid's house? Dude, not okay."

Wally shrugs. "He deserved it."

"What did he do?"

Wally glares at Sid. "He knows what he did."

I tug on Wally's shirt. "But I don't."

"Rumor has it Sid called you a nasty word," Hailey says.

"Oh?" I stare at Sid until he starts squirming.

"Snot bad," Sid says and then waves to everyone before high-tailing it out of the bar.

Hailey claps. "Awesome! Can you teach me your stare? The uncles refuse to teach me how to stare someone down." She pauses and her nose scrunches. "You're standing in Wally's arms." She gasps. "Oh my god, it's finally happening. Uncle Wally is falling in love."

I feel my face heat, but I refuse to let it happen. Instead, I use my go-to trick to stop a blush, I think of something funny. It's easy. The face Wally made when I placed the muzzle of my handgun at his temple when he didn't realize I was behind him is freaking hilarious. I end up smirking instead of blushing.

"No one's falling in love," I declare.

"Love? Who's in love?" Phoebe asks as she arrives with Ryker in tow.

I ignore her question to ask, "How did it go in Fond du Lac? Did you find the evidence to prove Mr. Dithers is trying to scam his insurance company?"

Fond du Lac is a small town about an hour north of Milwaukee. Phoebe drove there yesterday after I discovered Mr. Dithers has a job in the town working on a construction crew, which is mighty suspicious considering the guy was 'injured' on the job at a local construction site and hasn't been able to return to work due to 'back pain'.

"Dithers is an idiot. I had a picture of him carrying a five-gallon drum of paint within an hour."

I cock an eyebrow. "You were gone two days."

She blushes and her gaze drops to her shoes. Ah. "We were—"

I lift my hand. "No explanation needed."

Hailey slaps my hand out of the air. "Speak for yourself. I want an explanation."

Aiden palms her neck. "Honey, we've talked about this."

"Correction. You talked about this. I didn't."

Before Aiden can respond, Phoebe speaks. "Why are Wally and Chrissie all cozied up?"

This is getting ridiculous. Is it comfy being in Wally's arms? Yes. Does he make me safe? He does. Is there any chance of anything happening between us? N. O. No. I pull away from Wally, but he doesn't let me.

"I like you in my arms," he grumbles into my ear.

Phoebe rubs her hands together. "Finally! I'm going to win a bet."

"Bet? What bet?" I ask, although I have a sneaking suspicion I know exactly what she's talking about.

Wally and his brothers will bet on absolutely everything, including other people's relationships. From what I heard, Lenny upgraded his motorbike after he won all the bets regarding Phoebe and Ryker's relationship.

Phoebe bites her lip. "Um…"

I turn my stare on Barney. If anyone's going to break, it's him. The goofball doesn't stand a chance. His eyes widen and he throws his hands up in front of his face. "Make it stop! Make it stop!"

I switch to Lenny, but he smirks and motions at me to bring it on. Crap. I can't use my stare on Phoebe or Hailey when their men are around. I like my skin attached my body, thank you very much.

Wally whirls me around to face him. "Don't let them get to you, Angel. It's none of their business how our relationship proceeds and how quickly."

"I think you mean *if* we decide to enter a relationship."

His response? A smirk. My nostrils flare, but before I can speak, Phoebe shouts, "This is going to be awesome!"

Awesome? Not likely. Painful is the word I think she's searching for, because relationships are pain, plain and simple.

Chapter 7

I discovered my boyfriend is a communist spy. I
guess I should have noticed sooner, but I chose to
ignore the red flags.

I STOMP UP THE sidewalk to Wally's house. I can't believe the
asshole broke into my house. Who the hell does he think he is?
He promised me he would stop digging into my background.
It's been one day. One single freaking day. And he's already
broken his promise. Typical man. Men don't understand the
meaning of the word promise.

Nothing about this house screams Wally. It's a ranch house
in the suburbs for goodness sake. Wally should be living in a
cave somewhere not out in the open like a normal civilian. Of
course, this is how spooks live. Out in the open like they have
nothing to hide. Sure, they don't.

I debate knocking on the door for approximately two seconds
before trying the handle and finding it unlocked. Uh oh. I reach
for my weapon. There's no way Wally's door would be unlocked
unless he's got trouble.

I plaster myself to the side of the entry before peeking around the door jam. Wally's standing in the middle of the living room with his hands crossed over his chest, waiting for me.

"A deaf person could have heard you coming up the sidewalk."

I holster my weapon before entering his house. Now, this is the kind of place I expected Wally to have. It's an open concept with the living room in front and the kitchen to the rear. The floors are a dark hardwood, and the furniture is sleek black leather. The kitchen has marble countertops and shiny gray cabinets. Yep, this place fits Wally to a T.

"I wasn't trying to disguise my arrival," I snarl.

"What's crawled up your ass? You were sweet as a kitten less than an hour ago, Angel."

Angel. How dare you call me angel after what he did!

"Because you broke your promise to me," I snarl. "You couldn't help yourself, could you?"

He freezes. "What are you talking about?"

"You're going to deny it?" I huff. This man is unbelievable. Un-freaking-believable.

He holds up his hands in surrender. "I promise. I don't know what you're talking about."

Promise? Does the man know what the word means? I shut my response off and study his body language. He appears open and unguarded as if he's telling the truth. Of course, the man has probably been taught to lie from the best teachers our government has to offer.

I observe him closely as I announce, "Someone broke into my place."

His body vibrates with anger. "Were you in the house? Are you okay? Were you injured?"

I hold up a hand to stop his barrage of questions. "I wasn't home."

His shoulders deflate and he strides toward me. I shake my head. "Tell me it wasn't you."

He scowls. "Do you have to ask?"

I roll my eyes. "Were you or were you not the same man who was sneaking around my house last night?"

He sighs. "I promise it wasn't me." I study him, but I can't tell if he's lying. "I'm not lying. I will never lie to you." I snort, and he grins. "I admit I won't always tell you everything about my work, because I can't, but I will never lie to you."

When I don't say anything, he shuffles forward and grasps my hands in his. "At some point, you have to decide to trust someone. You can't live behind those walls you've erected forever."

I'm perfectly happy living behind my walls. The one time I let them down, it nearly destroyed me. Nearly? It did destroy me. I've had to rebuild everything.

"I'm not him," Wally snaps.

My heart stalls in my chest. "Him? What are you talking about?"

He drops my hands to cradle my face. "I know someone hurt you bad. It's plain to see in everything you do."

My heart commences beating again. He doesn't know what happened. Thank you, lord! I don't want anyone to know what a complete and utter fool I was.

"Now, what happened tonight? You left the bar less than an hour ago."

I left McGraw's early as I was feeling mighty uncomfortable with how familiar Wally was acting. Well, not exactly. I was feeling uncomfortable with how comfortable I was in Wally's arms. Shit. I'm doing it again. I'm standing here with him a breath away his hands caressing my face.

I clear my throat and retreat forcing Wally to drop his hands. "Can I get a glass of water?"

He goes to the kitchen and pours me a glass of water. When he returns, he motions to a chair. "Sit. Tell me what happened." He pauses. "Please."

Since he's being reasonable and not pushy, I don't scowl at him. I do nearly finish my water before telling him what happened, though.

"I returned home from the bar to discover one of my fail-safes was disturbed."

I don't tell him the fail-safe was a piece of clear tape on my door. I don't trust the man after all.

"And your security system?"

"Didn't go off. No signs of forced entry on the door."

"And you're certain your fail-safe was disturbed?"

I don't bother answering his question. If he wants me to trust him, he's going to need to trust me. This is not a one-way street.

"Do you think someone was in your house?"

"No. I think …" I pause. Do I trust this man enough to tell him my theories? What the hell. It's not like he doesn't have the same theories.

"I think someone was either disturbed while trying to break in – maybe they saw my security system – or …" This is the part I don't want to admit. "someone's screwing with me."

To his credit, Wally doesn't gloat about my giving him a bit of my trust. "Do you have any idea who could be screwing with you?"

"No idea." I'm serious. My past can't be coming back to bite me in the ass because my past is dead. As in blown to smithereens. Ka-boom!

Wally studies me for a long time. Just when I think he's going to let it go, he stands and sits on the coffee table in front of my chair. "What about the guy?"

"What guy?"

He frowns. "Don't be flippant. You know what guy I'm talking about."

I don't speak. I'm not explaining my sad history to him. I gave him the story about my parents. It's more than I've given anyone in a while. It's more than I expected to ever give anyone again.

"Me and my brothers can protect you. But we need to know what to watch for. What trouble you're in."

I blow out a puff of air. Not this again. "I'm not in trouble. I'm not in danger. If you didn't try to breach my house, then it must have been a burglar." Why the hell did I say someone might be messing with me? Stupid. Stupid. Stupid.

He doesn't let it go. Of course, he doesn't. The man is stubborn with a capital S. "We've helped other people. We saved Phoebe when her husband came after her. We helped get Faith clear of the gangs in Saint Louis. We can help you, too."

Gangs in Saint Louis? I would have never thought Faith got caught up with gangs. The woman is as wholesome as apple pie.

"I'm positive it's a burglary gone wrong." It has to be. "No one's targeting me. I promise. I'm not lying."

Wally stares at me for a moment before giving in. "I'll talk to Aiden. He can check if there's been an increase in home burglaries in your area."

Hailey's husband is a detective in the robbery division of the police department. I hope there's been an increase in robberies in my area because I fear Wally will use the 'break-in' at my place as an excuse for him to renege on his promise to not dig into my past.

I stand. "Sounds good. I'm off. "

He captures my wrist before I can make my escape. "There's no reason to leave. We can watch a movie together or have a drink."

"No thanks. I'm tired."

He drops my wrist. "And you need time to fortify your walls."

I don't deny it. I'd be lying and I'm saving my lies to this man for when I truly need them.

"You going to be okay sleeping in your house now?"

Is he serious? I'm perfectly safe in my house. I've got security measures on top of security measures. And, if all else fails, I have a 9 mm in my bedside drawer and a shotgun under the bed. It's not as if I need the weapons, I'm pretty damn good in hand-to-hand combat if I do say so myself.

"I'm good."

He escorts me to the door, but before I manage to get away, he palms my neck and leans down to kiss my forehead.

"Sleep tight, Angel."

"You need to stop calling me angel."

He smirks. "I'll stop calling you angel as soon as you stop liking it."

Son of a bitch. I can't deny I enjoy someone thinking I'm an angel. I'm not. Not even close. Even if I argue the things I've done were in the name of freedom, they were still actions an angel should never perform.

I open the door and wave as I leave. As I drive home, I mentally add enjoying hearing Wally call me angel to the list of things I need to fortify my walls against.

Chapter 8

What do you call a janitor who works at spy headquarters? A sweeper agent.

I SMOOTH OUT MY frown before entering the wedding boutique. Faith is shopping for her wedding dress today and somehow I've been invited. I don't know why. If I'm forced to, I'll admit Hailey and Phoebe are my friends, but I barely know Faith. I can count on one hand the number of conversations I've had with her.

Suzie skips as she approaches me. "Please don't skip," I tell her. "Grayson will lose his mind if he finds out."

"Finds out? Why would he find out? You're not a snitch, are you?"

A snitch. Not likely. I'm honest and reliable. Although, in my past life, I may have cozied up to people to learn their secrets. Secrets I then told to my superiors. Crap. Maybe I am a snitch.

Suzie threads her arm through mine. "Come. They have champagne. Since I can't drink, I need to drink vicariously through you."

We join the group in the back room. In addition to Suzie, Hailey, Phoebe, and Valerie are here. Faith must be trying on a gown as she's not in the room.

"I don't know why I'm here," I mumble as I sip the champagne Suzie thrust in my hand.

"Duh." Suzie rolls her eyes. "You're one of the crew now."

Hailey waggles her eyebrows. "Because Wally's my uncle and you're my soon-to-be-aunt."

"What?" Faith screeches as she dashes out of a dressing room wearing a puffy gown. "When's the big day? How did he propose?"

"Who cares how he proposed? I want to hear about how Wally is in the sack. The man looks like he knows all the secrets to satisfy a woman." Valerie licks her lips.

Suzie lifts a hand. "High five!" The two smack their hands together before turning their attention my way. "Well? We want all the deets."

Phoebe groans. "Oh no. There are two of them now."

"I know!" Suzie shouts. "Isn't it awesome? Her crazy matches mine. I'm sorry Hailey, but I've got a new BFF."

I clear my throat. "Perhaps we could concentrate on Faith. It is her big day."

Faith sighs before plopping down on one of the sofas. "Then, you're not marrying Wally?"

"Of course not. We haven't even kissed."

Shit. I regret the words the minute they're out. Now they're going to think I'm thinking about kissing Wally. I mean, I am. Who wouldn't want to kiss the man? Every time his lips touch my forehead, I want to grab his head and plaster his lips to mine. But I don't want these women to know those thoughts. I'm not the type who gabs to girlfriends about boys.

"Who's confused?" Suzie searches the room. "Because I most certainly am. The two were all cozied up at McGraw's last night and he calls her angel."

"And," Hailey adds, "word on the street has it she was at his house last night."

I narrow my eyes at her. "Your husband has a big mouth."

"He does." She winks. Not what I meant, and she knows it.

"Details!" Suzie and Valerie scream in unison.

"Shush," Faith orders. "They'll kick us out of here and I need to pick a dress."

A change of topic. I latch onto it. "Why are you picking a dress this soon? You got engaged a week ago."

"Pops isn't waiting to marry her," Hailey explains. "He wants her to have his last name yesterday. He threatened to have a courthouse wedding if she wasn't prepared to marry him by Valentine's Day."

Valerie leans forward and whisper-shouts. "Is Pops this bossy everywhere? Like in bed maybe?"

Phoebe groans. "No, no, no. We are not talking about what Pops is like in bed."

"What's your problem?" Valerie asks. "He's not your dad, and the man is a stone-cold fox."

"But he's like a dad to her since her own dad is a total dickhead," Suzie explains.

"I'm glad I booked a double appointment. We're never going to find a wedding gown for me."

Hailey motions toward Phoebe. "No need to worry. Ask Phoebe to help. The woman is a fashion savant. She'll have a gown perfect for your figure picked out in no time flat."

Faith bats her lashes at Phoebe. "Would you mind?"

Phoebe sets down her orange juice and gets to her feet. She's a bit pale this morning. Of course, she's probably not feeling great since she's obviously pregnant. I'm surprised Suzie hasn't caught on yet.

"Of course not."

Faith flings herself at Phoebe and they nearly fall to the floor. I stand to steady Phoebe. I don't know much about pregnant women, but I'm not letting my pregnant friend get crushed to the floor.

"Why are you helping Phoebe?" Suzie asks. "She doesn't need your help. Faith's a skinny thing. Phoebe can handle her."

I cock an eyebrow at Phoebe. It's up to her if she's ready to tell everyone. Hailey thinks differently. She squeals and shouts. "Are we telling now?"

Suzie's eyes widen before she jumps to her feet. "Whoo-hoo! I'm not the only one with a bun in the oven."

"You're pregnant?" Phoebe nods at Faith's question, and Faith wraps her up tight in a hug. The two sway back and forth. "I'm happy for you. You're going to be a great mom."

Tears leak from Phoebe's eyes, and I grab some tissues from the box on the table. I guess it's normal for women to cry when trying on wedding gowns since there are several boxes scattered around the room.

Phoebe wipes at her eyes. "I'm still terrified. Ryker and I know literally nothing about how to be good parents."

Faith squeezes her arms. "No one does, but you figure it out along the way." She motions to the rest of us. "And you've got a great support system to help you."

"And Pops will be happy to help out with his grandchild."

Faith blushes at her words. "Thank you for sharing your dad with me." The tears fall faster as she rushes Hailey and hugs her.

Hailey pats her back. "Pops always wanted a big family." She smiles over at Faith. "And now he's finally got the family he always deserved."

I hand out tissues and glasses of champagne and orange juice as the women gather themselves together. I'm not much for public displays of affection, but I know myself well enough to admit I'm a bit jealous of how close these women are to each other.

I end up sitting on a sofa next to Valerie. "Are you re-thinking your decision to have an extended vacation in Milwaukee now?"

"No way. After everything Faith's been through in Saint Louis, first with her asshole ex, then with the gangs and Ollie, I'm happy to sit here and observe while she gets everything her heart desires." She leans close to whisper. "I am ready for the tears to end, though. Can we get on with the drinking and shenanigans now?"

I bark out a laugh. When my laughter dies off, I realize everyone's staring at me. "What?" I peer down at my clothes to check for stains, but there is none.

"I don't think I've ever heard you laugh before," Faith says.

I roll my eyes. "We've known each other a minute. I laugh."

Hailey shakes her head. "No, you smirk and appear amused. You don't laugh."

"Whatever."

"I got you, girl," Valerie whispers before standing. "I have some ideas for the wedding I'd like to discuss."

"We're not doing a big wedding. We're getting married at the church and then a small reception at McGraw's."

"There's goes my idea for a food truck," Valerie mumbles.

Suzie rubs her stomach. "I could go for a food truck right now."

Valerie ignores her. "On the other hand, a bar does scream wedding day beer pong."

Faith swallows. "Beer pong?"

"Tell me you're at least doing the traditional garter throw. I read an article about attaching a garter to a football and throwing it. Sounds like fun."

Suzie giggles. "Can you imagine the uncles going after a football?"

Hailey motions to me. "As if we don't know Pops is going to give the garter to Uncle Wally."

I hold my hands up. "What is it with you guys and wanting to set me up with Wally? The man is nearly sixty and he's never been married, there must be a reason."

"Maybe he's never met the right woman before," Phoebe suggests.

I wag a finger at her. "No. Just because you're loved up and pregnant doesn't mean you get to start matching all your friends off. It's part of the rule book."

"What rule book? Is there a rule book?" Suzie appears genuinely confused.

Hailey squeezes her shoulder. "She doesn't mean an actual book. She means the rules of the sisterhood."

"Huh." Suzie taps her chin. "I didn't think Chrissie would be big on rules."

"Why not?" I mean, I'm not, but why would she think I'm a rulebreaker?

She shrugs. "Anyone who can resist Wally when he's got his sights set on her is not a rule follower."

I have no idea what the one has to do with the other. "You just wanted to bring me and Wally together up again, didn't you?"

She shoots her finger like it's a gun. "Got it!"

"I think it's time we got back to finding Faith a wedding gown."

"A wedding dress!" Faith shouts.

"Okay." I nod before raising my eyebrow and leveling the group with a stare. This one clearly communicates I mean business.

"Mean Chrissie is here," Suzie pouts but she takes a seat.

"I'll find some gowns for Faith to try on," Phoebe announces before scurrying off.

Faith returns to the dressing room, and Valerie follows her.

Hailey grasps my arm. "Seriously. You need to teach me how you do the stare."

I wink at her. Anything to get the topic off of Wally and me, because this woman is not ready to let her walls down no matter how much Wally comes at them with a sledgehammer.

Chapter 9

Dave: "My dad says you're spying on us!"
Zuckerberg: "He's not your dad."

I RE-ADJUST THE BOX with the brand-new coffee machine in my arms when I hear the elevator ding to indicate I've reached the floor of the *We Cheat, You Eat* offices. Since it's Monday morning before eight, the corridor is deserted. I balance the box on my knee as I dig around for my keys.

I hear something crash to the ground behind the door. Shit. The offices have been breached. I let go of the box to draw my weapon. I cringe at the sound of the box hitting the floor. Whoever is in the office can't have missed the racket. Damn. I've given away my position.

My nine in my right hand, I place my left hand on the door. I twist and discover it unlocked just as I suspected it would be. I rush through the door with my weapon raised. There's no one in the reception area, but that's no guarantee I'm alone. I proceed quickly through the rooms to clear them.

Once I've established the two offices, filing room, and re-stroom are indeed empty, I holster my weapon and call Hailey before returning to the hallway to pick up the box I'd dropped.

When Hailey rushes inside fifteen minutes later, I'm fiddling with the coffee machine. I must have broken a piece when I dropped it because the stupid thing isn't working like it should be.

"Are you all right?" Hailey drops the leashes for her dogs, Lola and Leroy, before dragging me away from the machine and into her arms.

I pat her back twice. It's a bit awkward since until I met her and her friends, I hadn't hugged a friend in decades. "I'm fine. The place was unlocked but empty when I arrived. Nothing appears to have been stolen, but a lamp from your desk broke. I'm assuming it's the crash I heard when I arrived."

She groans. "Aiden is going to become a great big worrywart again."

"There's no need to tell him. Nothing happened."

She opens her mouth to answer but shuts it again when Leroy barks from inside her office. I draw my weapon and rush to her office. I swear I cleared the room. I checked under her desk and behind the curtains. I'm not an idiot.

Leroy is in the corner growling at the filing cabinet. "What's up, boy?" I ask. His response? Another growl.

"Get the dogs," I order Hailey.

She grabs Leroy's collar and drags him away while whistling for Lola to follow her. Once the door shuts behind them, I kneel in front of the cabinet. I probably look like an idiot pointing a gun at a cabinet, but my motto is 'better a safe idiot than a proud dead woman'.

Something rushes out of the cabinet and streaks past me before jumping onto the desk. I rush after it before realizing it's a tiny kitten. A gray, fluffy kitten to be exact. I holster my weapon before approaching it with my hands out.

"Here, kitty, kitty," I murmur before my hand darts out, and I nab the kitten by the scruff of its neck.

"I think I've caught the culprit," I say as I open the door into the reception area. As soon as I enter the area, Leroy goes mad. He barks and stands on his hind legs to get at the kitten. "Down!"

The dog whines before dropping to his belly. "I'll lock the doggies in my office until Aiden gets here."

"You called Aiden?"

She shrugs. "It is what it is."

The door opens, and Phoebe and Ryker stroll in. Phoebe's eyes widen when she notices the kitten in my arms. In my arms? Dang it. I'm snuggling the critter now.

"You brought a cat to the office when Hailey has two dogs? I knew you were brave, but this is ridiculous."

Ryker examines the area before grunting, "What happened?"

"Door was unlocked when I arrived, nothing disturbed except for the lamp I suspect this little guy broke when he jumped on the desk."

Phoebe gasps. "Someone broke into the offices?"

Ryker doesn't respond. He marches to the office he shares with Phoebe to confirm for himself nothing's missing. The guy locks up all his files every single time he leaves the office. I'd call him paranoid, but I'm the same way.

"Are you okay?" Phoebe asks as she extends her hand to pet the kitten. The kitty snarls at her before dipping her head to nuzzle my arm. "Huh. I guess kittens don't love me the way dogs do. Are you going to keep her?"

"We always had cats growing up," I mumble as I scratch the kitty's head.

"Oh yeah, where did you grow up?" Suzie asks.

I don't startle at her sudden appearance as I heard her clomping down the hallway. "What are you doing here?" I ask instead of answering her question.

The woman is super nosy, and it's entirely too fun to rile her up. Where I grew up is no secret. I grew up in Sheboygan, a town about an hour north of Milwaukee on Lake Michigan.

"Hailey called."

"Who didn't you call?" I ask Hailey as she shuts the door to her office behind her.

"Suzie is still my business partner, although she no longer works here. Of course, I'm going to call her when the offices have been broken into."

"You bought a coffee maker," Suzie squeals, and the cat hisses at her.

"I don't know why you didn't buy one earlier. I did the calculations and it's much cheaper to buy a coffee maker – even a fancy one to make all those frou-frou drinks Phoebe likes – than it is to dash down to the coffee shop constantly. And it's better for the environment. No more single use to-go cups."

Hailey lifts her hand for a high-five. "Thanks for proving hiring you was the right choice."

I stare at her hand until she drops it. I'm forty-nine years old, I don't high-five about coffee makers.

"Except I dropped it and broke it."

"I'll check it out." Suzie starts pressing all kinds of buttons on the machine.

I move to stop her, but Hailey places a hand on my arm. "Leave her be. Believe it or not, klutzy girl is good with machines."

"It's the brewing thing," Suzie says as she fiddles with the machine. "I've had to learn to fix my equipment to save money."

"Save money?" Phoebe asks. "I thought Shorty's Brewing Sensation was doing well."

I hear feet pounding in the hallway, and I round my desk to sit down. Aiden rushes into the room three seconds later.

"Are you okay? Are you hurt?" Aiden pats Hailey down like she's a suspect as he scans her for supposed injuries.

Hailey shoves him away. "One, I wasn't here. Chrissie was." He glances my way and I wave at him. "Two, nothing happened. A cat climbed through my window is all."

I clear my throat. "Except I checked your window was closed before I left on Friday afternoon, and the front door was unlocked."

Hailey throws her arms in the air. "I thought you didn't want to involve the police."

"I didn't, but they're here now and I'm not lying to them." I nod to the two uniformed officers standing in the doorway.

"You okay?" Aiden asks me.

As if I'm scared of a little intruder. "I'm fine."

He nods and motions for the uniformed police to enter. "The officers will take your statement."

"Got it."

Aiden kisses Hailey's forehead. "If you're okay, I need to get back to work." She shoos him on his way.

I spend the next thirty minutes answering the same question posed fifty different ways. Phoebe and Hailey don't leave me alone the entire time. I give them the look a few times, but they keep their eyes averted to avoid its impact.

"You better call Wally," Phoebe says after the police leave.

"Wally? Why would I call Wally?" He has nothing to do with the business.

I hear the sound of grinding coffee before Suzie throws her hands in the air. "Yes! I fixed it." The coffee finishes brewing, and she grabs the cup, but before she can take a sip, Phoebe steals it out of her hands.

"No coffee for the pregnant lady."

Ryker appears at the door and nabs the coffee cup from Phoebe. He grunts before swallowing the espresso in one sip. Phoebe slaps his arm. "You stole my coffee."

He cocks an eyebrow. "Pregnant, remember?"

Her eyes light up and her hands travel to her still flat belly. "Oh, yeah."

Ryker nods at me. "And you. Call Wally," he orders before marching back to his office.

I don't bother responding to him. Ryker can look as tough as he wants – and he does look pretty tough at six-foot-six with a thick beard – but he can't order me around.

"If you're not going to call Wally, can you at least videotape his actions when he arrives at your house tonight?" Hailey asks.

Phoebe rubs her hands together. "Great idea."

"Or I could hang cameras up in her living room," Suzie suggests.

I point to her. "You need to get back to work. Grayson has called at least five times since you've been here."

She removes her phone from her pocket. Her eyes widen as she reads her messages. "How did you know?"

Because I heard the phone ring five times. I don't answer her, though. Better to let her think I have some sort of secret power.

"Are you like Wally? A super-secret spy?"

I chuckle. "Is Wally really a super-secret spy if you know about it?"

"Huh. Good point." The phone in her hand rings. "I better go. Enjoy your coffee." She bows and smacks her head with her phone. "Ow." She rubs her forehead as she leaves.

Phoebe sighs and stands. "I guess I'll get to work if you're not going to call Wally."

Hailey grunts in agreement.

I ignore them. They are obviously confused about my relationship with Wally. No. Not a relationship. Flipping hell. I hope I'm not lying to myself.

Chapter 10

I told my wife I think all our electrical items are spying on us. "Nonsense," she said. I laughed. She laughed. Siri laughed. Alexa laughed. The toaster laughed.

WALLY

I prepare myself for a fight before I knock on Chrissie's door. The door opens a second later. She obviously saw me coming.

"Knocking on the door this time? You positive you don't want to sneak around the perimeter of my house for a little while first?" she asks with a smile on her face.

I'll let her make fun of me all day and night if it results in her smiling. The woman is pretty but when she smiles, her blue eyes light up and she becomes absolutely gorgeous. My lips tip up before I can stop them. Witnessing this woman happy makes me happy. I'd do anything to make her happy, including get into a fight about her safety.

"Do you need to tell me something, Angel?"

The smile drops from her face, and she crosses her arms over her chest. "Why would I need to tell you anything?"

"Because I can't keep you safe if I don't know about any threats."

Her eyes narrow and she glares at me. "I don't need you to keep me safe. I can keep myself safe. I think I proved my competence already."

I am never going to hear the end of her getting the drop on me when I was canvassing her house. And I've made my peace with it. As long as she's here to give me shit. She can't give me shit, though, if whoever's threatening her is successful.

"No one's threatening me."

I cock an eyebrow. "Really? Someone broke into your house, and someone broke into your office at work."

"One, no one actually broke into my house. And two, I don't have an office. It's Hailey's business. There's absolutely no proof the break-in was targeted at me."

I prowl toward her. "You know damn well two break-ins—" When she opens her mouth to correct me, I hold out my hand to stop her. "One attempted break-in and one break-in within a few days isn't a coincidence."

She doesn't respond. She can't. She knows I'm right. I might not have been in many relationships in my life, but I know better than to say I'm right out loud. I wait for her to give in. Of course, she doesn't. Not my Chrissie. Stubborn is the woman's middle name.

"Can we hurry this up?" I urge. "I need to get your new alarm system installed before dinner, and I have a seven o'clock reservation." Hurt flashes in her eyes. "With you, Angel, a dinner reservation with you."

She stiffens. "I never said I was going to dinner with you. In fact, you never asked."

I cup her face with my hand. "Angel, will you have dinner with me?"

"We can eat together, but it doesn't mean anything. I don't do relationships."

I wink. "I'll wear you down."

She huffs. "You're welcome to try."

Game on, Angel. Game on.

I bend forward and kiss her forehead. She tries to hide it, but I notice how her body leans toward me as if she can't help herself. I swallow my smile. Gloating will get me nowhere with her.

"Now, kindly move out of my way. I need to install this new alarm system."

"I don't need a new alarm system."

I don't respond. I'm going to install this new system whether she likes it or not. I prefer to do it with her consent, but I can always come back when she's at work and install it then.

After a few moments of staring at each other, she motions to her system. "Go ahead."

I enter her hallway and make my way to her security panel. She's not lying. This is a top-of-the-line system. I wouldn't expect anyone in this neighborhood at this price point of house to have this type of system. And yet, she claims she's not in danger. The mystery of Chrissie continues. A mystery I'm determined to solve.

I turn to confront Chrissie about her system and notice she's standing in the middle of the living room cradling a kitten. This must be the kitten she found in Hailey's office this morning.

"You kept the kitty?" I examine her living room and discover a scratching post in the corner, a water and food bowl on the kitchen floor, and a cat bed. This explains why she wasn't at the gym this afternoon.

Her attention is riveted on the tiny animal as she answers. "She needed a home." She kisses the top of its furry head. "Didn't you?" she asks the kitty as she scratches her head.

"What are you going to name her?" I ask.

"Gray."

I hold out a hand. "Can I hold her?"

She shrugs. "It's your funeral."

I grasp Gray by the back of her neck and bring her close to cuddle her. "Have you had her examined by the vet yet?"

When Chrissie doesn't answer, I glance up to find her gaping at me. "What? I like cats. Dogs are too much work and I'm gone too much for one anyway, but a cat is easy to maintain."

She clears her throat. "I have an appointment at the vet tomorrow."

"Good." I hand her Gray. "Get her settled and then we can head to dinner."

She smirks. "You aren't going to install a new security system?"

"Stop being a smartass. You know it's not necessary." I can admit when I'm wrong, but I'm not going to let her rub it in.

After she settles Gray in her bed, she stands and brushes her hands on her jeans. "I'm ready. Let's get this over with."

Chrissie is my kind of woman. She isn't going to spend an hour primping to get ready to leave the house. She doesn't need to. Chrissie in jeans and a button-down shirt is perfection. My hands itch to get a handful of her curves in them. It'll happen. Patience is the name of the game.

I watch as she arms the alarm system before we leave the house. When she heads toward her car, I stop her with a hand on her lower back and guide her toward my truck. As if I'll allow her to drive herself to our first date. And make no mistake about it, this is our first date.

Chrissie laughs as I escort her inside the all-you-can-eat steak house. "I should have known you wouldn't go for romance."

I maneuver her until I can peer into her eyes. "Angel, I will give you all the romance you want, but I know you. If I had brought you to a romantic restaurant, you would have snuck out the back door." Where I would have been waiting for her.

"I wouldn't have snuck out the back door," she scoffs. "I'd have marched straight out the front door."

I chuckle. Bold and brassy has never come in such a pretty package before. The hostess escorts us to a booth in the rear of the restaurant, far away from other people. We order beers and she slaps the menus down on the table before leaving.

Chrissie rubs her hands together. "I'm going to eat my weight in meat. No silly salad bar for me. I'll get my money's worth."

"You aren't paying," I snap.

"Yeah, I am. I said I'd pay since you put in my alarm system."

When did we agree to this? It doesn't matter. "I didn't put in the new alarm system."

She shrugs. "I can't help it you didn't realize I didn't need a new alarm system when we made the deal I'd pay."

If she thinks she can talk circles around me, she's got another thing coming. "The agreement was you'd come to dinner with me. I asked you, I'm paying."

She opens her mouth to start another argument, but the waitress arrives with our beers. After we order and the waitress leaves, she opens her mouth again but I'm not having it.

I reach across the table to grasp her hand. I squeeze it as I explain, "Angel, when I ask a woman to eat with me, I pay."

"Do you ask a lot of women to dinner?"

I cough to stop the smile from forming on my face. She's jealous of non-existent women. I don't care what she says about not doing relationships, Chrissie and I are doing this.

"You're the first woman I've asked to dinner in over two decades."

"Geez, Wally. How old are you?"

I don't hesitate to answer. "I'm fifty-nine."

"You're ancient. What was it like eating with the dinosaurs?" she teases.

"Terrifying," I tell her.

She giggles. "I doubt I need to tell you my age, but let's pretend you don't know. I'm forty-nine."

Of course, I already know her age. I ran a preliminary background check on her the night I met her. And it wasn't because I thought she was in Milwaukee to bring trouble to Max and his family. The second I saw Chrissie I wanted her, but I can't jump in bed with an unknown woman. Not with my job.

"A baby," I say with a wink.

"I want to hear all about how you and your brothers met. I know you were in the same Army unit but when did you meet? Was Barney always a jokester? And did Sid really pick up a man dressed in a hijab in the desert?"

"Get this," I start and go on to tell her the story of how Barney tricked Sid into picking up a man.

"I'm stuffed," Chrissie groans some time later. "I'm unbuttoning the top button of my jeans and you're going to pretend to not notice despite noticing every single thing happening all the time."

"I don't see a thing." I finish my beer and stand. "Come on. Let's go for a walk to help us work off the steak."

Chrissie takes my hand and I help her to her feet. "I don't think you can walk off ten gazillion calories."

"Ten gazillion? I guess you got your money's worth after all."

I wrap my arm around her, and we exit the restaurant to discover snow falling to the ground. Chrissie gazes up at the sky. "Man, I missed the snow. I vote snowstorm over sandstorm any day of the week."

I file away the tidbit about sandstorms for another day. Tonight, I'm not going to dig into her past. Tonight is for getting to know each other the old-fashioned way. And the more I get to know Chrissie, the more I want to know. This woman has me wrapped around her little finger and she hasn't a clue.

Chapter 11

What did the spy say to his informant in the cornfield? Careful there are ears all around us.

I sigh when Phoebe and Hailey plop down in the chairs across from my desk on Tuesday morning. "Can I help you?"

"Why are you smiling?" Hailey demands.

I frown. "I'm not smiling."

"Not right now, but you've been smiling like a madwoman all morning."

I'm not telling her I'm smiling because I can't stop thinking about what a good time I had with Wally last night. "I'm confused. Am I not allowed to smile?"

Hailey rolls her eyes. "Naturally, you're allowed to smile, but you usually don't."

"Are you saying I'm normally grumpy?"

She throws her arms in the air. "Phoebe, you talk to her."

"No way. She'll give me the eye and before I know what's happening, I'll be confessing to the time I put Nair in my college roommate's shampoo bottle."

Phoebe pulled a prank on someone? This I gotta hear. "What did she do to you?"

"Eek! This is exactly what I mean! She didn't even give me the eye and I'm telling her all my secrets."

Ryker grunts from inside his office. Apparently, Phoebe can interpret his grunts because she yells at him, "Don't worry. I won't tell her about our sexy times, big guy."

While Ryker is one hot dude, I don't want to hear about him and Phoebe getting it on. I am not the kind of woman who wants to hear about her friends having sex. Actually, I'm not the kind of woman who usually has friends. Or, at least, not many.

My phone buzzes, and I flip it over. Lexi is calling. Speaking of friends. I stand.

"I need to answer this," I say and leave before Hailey or Phoebe can respond.

I answer the phone while in the hallway. "Give me ten seconds." I need to be in a secure location for this call. I hurry down the stairs and outside to my car. Once I'm in the car with the doors locked, I pick up the phone again.

"Hi, Lexi. Thanks for calling me back."

"Sorry it took me a couple days to get back to you."

I called Lexi on Friday night after the attempted break-in at my house. She's one of the few people who I trust to have my back.

"I understand." I don't bother with idle chitchat. I don't have the time for it. "I need to know if someone's digging into my background."

"Are you in trouble?"

"I don't know."

The sound of typing halts. "What do you mean you don't know? You're in Milwaukee, Wisconsin for gosh sakes. What the hell happens in Milwaukee?"

"I'll have you know Milwaukee has one of the highest crime rates in the country."

I sound like I'm bragging. I blame Lexi. She brings out the teenager in me. We might be friends, but we're competitive as hell with each other. It's not like Milwaukee is full of danger. For the most part, it's like any other city – safe as long as you're careful and avoid certain areas.

She snorts. "As if you can't handle a common criminal."

"Don't insult me. Of course, I can handle a common criminal." It's true. The training I underwent on Uncle Sam's dime is the best in the world.

"But I don't think a common criminal is behind what's happening."

"Fill me in."

I tell her about the attempted break-in at my house and the break-in at the PI firm.

"Nothing was stolen?"

"Nothing was disturbed. If the cat hadn't broken the lamp, I wouldn't have known someone had been inside the office."

"Except for the unlocked door."

"Except for the unlocked door," I repeat.

"Christina Lindberg, did you catch yourself a stalker?"

"I'm not worried about a stalker. I'm worried it's *him*." I don't need to spell out who I mean. Lexi knows.

"He's dead, isn't he? You saw the building he was in blow sky high."

I did, and I still re-live the building blowing up in my nightmares. "The body was never recovered."

"I haven't heard any talk of him being alive. He's not on any watch lists. And he would be if he were alive or suspected of being alive."

He sure as hell would be on every watch list in the Western World. It's what happens when you turn your back on your country and its allies.

"Let me do a bit of sniffing around." I feel the tension in my shoulders ease. She believes me. I'm not crazy. "I'm not saying it's him, but it sounds like there's something not right going on."

"Yeah, I have a bad feeling."

I denied it to Wally, but I do have a bad feeling. Call it a gut feeling, call it women's intuition, call it whatever you want, but I can't deny it. Something isn't sitting right with me.

"Damn. I'll make this a priority."

"Thanks," I say before ending the call.

I allow the door to my past that's been welded shut for my own sanity to open for a minute. Is it possible he's alive? I doubt it, but he wasn't working alone. It's possible one of his allies is around, but why would anyone target me? I'm out of the game. Not by choice. After what happened with him, I didn't have a choice.

Thinking about the past will get me nowhere. I shut the door to my past and weld it shut again before starting up my car.

Maybe if I pick up lunch for the office, Hailey and Phoebe won't grill me with a thousand questions about why I ran off when I got a phone call.

The rest of the day passes slowly at the office. Ryker and Phoebe head out to do some surveillance. Ryker won't let Phoebe out of his sight now she's pregnant. Thus far, she's letting him push her around, but I don't know how long it will last before she pushes back. I'm eagerly awaiting the explosion.

Aiden strolls into the office around four.

"Any news on the break-in?" I ask although I'm one-hundred percent convinced there's no news.

"It's low priority since nothing was stolen and there were no signs of forced entry."

I nod. I suspected as much.

He opens the door to Hailey's office and her dogs Lola and Leroy rush out. He gives them belly rubs before asking, "Can you dog sit them?"

"Nope."

"Don't be mean," Hailey shouts from inside her office.

"I'm not minding the dogs so you can have sex in your office. If you want to have sex, go home or go find a motel. Hell, I don't care if you do it in the back of a car, although not in the back of the company SUV because I am not cleaning up after you."

I don't blame her for wanting to have sex with Aiden whenever she has the chance. The man is gorgeous with his dark hair, square jaw, and blue eyes. Personally, I'm finding I prefer green eyes myself.

Hailey groans. "Don't be a clam jammer."

"Ew. Yuck. Please don't use that term ever again."

"Clam jam. Clam jam. Clam jam."

I jump to my feet and march to her office. Her eyes widen when she sees me, and she covers her face with her hands. "No! Don't give me the eye. I promise to stop using the term."

I smirk. Works every time. "Get out of here. Go home early."

"But the dogs whine and cry when we shut them out of the bedroom," she complains.

"Fine." I huff. "I'll mind the dogs. I'll bring them over to your house in an hour. But I better not glimpse any naked parts."

She bites her lip. "Make it two hours and you have a deal."

"Done. Get out of here."

She leaps out of her chair and rushes to Aiden who's standing in the doorway. She grabs his hand and tugs him toward the door. "Come on. Let's get out of here before she changes her mind or uses the eye on me." She shivers.

I follow them and shut the door behind them. Lola and Leroy stand at the door as if to follow Hailey and Aiden.

"Sorry doggies. Your momma and poppa need some alone time."

Lola whines and lays on her belly in front of the door. Leroy headbutts her before laying next to her.

Before I manage to sit down, my phone buzzes with a call from Lexi.

"You were quick," I say when I answer.

"Yeah, well, I wanted to warn you."

Shit. I was hoping my bad feeling was indigestion from eating my weight in red meat yesterday. "Tell me."

"Someone has been making inquiries about you."

"What kind of inquiries?"

"Trying to find out if you worked for the agency."

"No one should be able to get that information. Not after what happened in the Middle East."

"From what I can tell the information hasn't been accessed, but someone has been trying awful hard to access it."

Fucking Wally. He promised to stop digging into my past. I growl and the dogs' ears perk up as their heads swivel in my direction. I wave a hand at them, and they settle down.

"I have a lead on who it is."

"Keep me informed," Lexi orders before disconnecting.

I stand. I have someone I need to murder.

Chapter 12

A serial killer, car thief and Russian spy walks into a bar. And that was just the first guy.

I MARCH INTO McGRAW'S Bar where I know I'll find Wally thirty minutes later. If he's not off-grid, he practically lives at the bar. I motion for the dogs to follow me inside. Pops, Faith, and Ollie are sitting at a table enjoying an early dinner while Pepper, Ollie's brown lab puppy, lays under the table.

When the dogs notice Pepper, they run as fast as their four legs can to him, barking the entire way. As soon as they're in range, they do what all dogs do – sniff each other butts. Pepper's tail wags hard enough her entire butt is swaying back and forth. Apparently, the excitement is too much for her and she starts peeing.

"Ollie." Pops points to the dog and Ollie climbs to his feet.

"I know. I know. Let Pepper out." He grabs the dog's collar and drags her toward the back hallway leading to the tiny yard out back with Lola and Leroy following. Yard is pushing it. It's a patch of dirt barely large enough for a picnic table where the smokers hang out.

As soon as Pops notices me, he stands. When Faith tries to follow him, he shakes his head at her. She nods but waves to me while mouthing, *Are you okay?*

I grin to reassure her despite my anger being in the red zone – highly dangerous.

Pops doesn't bother greeting me. "What's wrong?" he asks as soon as he's within hearing range.

"I'm here to kill Wally."

Upon my announcement, Barney, Lenny, and Sid stand from their table and approach.

"This is going to be epic," Barney says while rubbing his hands together in anticipation.

Lenny smacks him upside the head. "Not now, goofball. This is serious."

Damn right this is serious. Wally's poking his nose where it doesn't belong. Breaking his promise to me is bad enough, but his curiosity is dangerous.

"What happened?" Sid asks. "Does Wally not satisfy you? I can give him some tips. The women never complain to me."

"Wally and I are not together."

Sid frowns. "Son of a bitch. Lenny's going to win another bet."

Lenny smirks. "I don't know why you insist on betting against me. You know I can't be beaten."

Wally strolls out of the back hallway. He smiles when his gaze lands on me. "Hey, Angel, I didn't know you were coming here tonight."

"Say goodbye to your brothers," I tell him.

"You want to head out? Let me grab my coat."

I shrug like it's all the same to me. "You want to grab your coat, go ahead. But it won't keep you warm as the last drop of blood drains from your body."

Barney clears his throat. "Maybe you shouldn't make threats in front of a room full of witnesses."

"One, it's not a threat. It's a promise. Two, you'll never find the body."

"Wisconsin case law allows conviction for murder without the body," Lenny points out. Isn't he helpful?

"What's going on?" Wally asks before I can answer Lenny.

"What's going? Like you don't know," I hiss.

Wally advances, but Pops blocks him from reaching me. "Maybe you should talk in my office."

I don't want to talk. I want to scream and shout before beating my fists against Wally until I can no longer feel his betrayal. I keep a lid on my emotions, though. I'm not giving my enemy any ammunition. And make no doubt about it, Wally is the enemy.

I'm not an idiot, though. I may be able to triumph over Wally individually, but there's no way I can fight all of his brothers at the same time. And I'm not stupid. I know they won't let me leave the bar with him.

"Fine, but I'm not cleaning up the blood."

I go to step around Pops, but he stops me with a hand on my arm. "You okay?"

"Don't worry. I promise to make this as painful as possible."

He drops his hand. "You need me, all you have to do is shout my name."

"I got this," I tell him before marching past Wally down the hallway. He reaches for my arm, but I lash out at him. "Don't you dare touch me." He raises his hands in surrender and follows me to the office.

Once we're in Pops' office and the door is shut behind us, I whirl around on Wally. "How could you? You promised? You're so full of bullshit, you're swimming in it."

His head cocks to the side as he observes me ranting. "Maybe you can explain what you're talking about."

I cross my arms over my chest and glare at him. "Are you going to stand there and deny it? I thought you were a better man. You'd think I'd learned my lesson by now."

"No," Wally snaps. "Be pissed all you want at me but don't compare me to him."

I freeze. Does he know? Lexi said my files remain sealed. How the hell did Wally find out?

"What do you know?" I manage to ask between grit teeth.

His hands move to cradle my face, but I don't want him touching me right now. I lean away from him, and he drops his hand with a sigh.

"I know someone hurt you. I know you don't trust men. I know every time you think I broke a promise to you, you lose your mind."

"Think you broke a promise?" I snarl. "I know you broke your promise. I know you went nosing around where you shouldn't have."

"Angel—"

"Don't call me that!" How dare he try to use a sweet nickname to soften me. I won't fall for it.

"I'll call you angel if I damn well want to."

"This conversation is a waste of time." I march to the door intent on leaving the city. I have a bug-out bag ready. I can be on a plane to anywhere in the world in less than an hour.

Wally grasps my upper arm. "You're not running away."

I whirl on him. "You don't get a say in my life. I don't allow people in my life who can't keep their promises."

Truth is I usually don't allow many people in my life at all. It's the way it is when you have the job I have. No. Had. Damn it. Things should be different now. I should be able to live a normal life. But Wally had to go and ruin it, didn't he?

"I promise I haven't done any research into you since I promised I would drop it."

I stand on my tiptoes and get in his face. "I don't believe you."

"I promise, but…" He pauses and I swear I can see a lightbulb switch on above his head.

I throw my arms in the air. "Here it comes."

He palms my neck and places his forehead against mine. My body loves the feel of him close to me, but I can't allow the feeling to affect how I handle things. I've been down this road before. Trusting how a man makes you feel is a direct path to betrayal. I try to retreat, but Wally squeezes my neck to hold me in place.

"I'm sorry. If I had known, I wouldn't have dug."

What does he think he knows? I'm afraid to ask, but fear does not rule me any more than squishy feelings about men. "Known what?"

He doesn't hesitate to hit me with the truth. "Known who your former employer was."

"My file is sealed," I say, and his eyes light up. Shit. I walked right into his trap.

"I won't press anymore as long as you promise me you're safe."

Not this again. "I can take care of myself."

"I know you can. I didn't ask you if you can take care of yourself. I asked if you're safe."

"I'm safe." I don't hesitate to answer. After all, he's dead. He must be dead. He has to be dead, right?

Wally wraps his arms around me and pulls me close until my body is flush with his. "Do you forgive me, Angel?"

Crap. I can hardly not forgive him. After all, he did keep his promise. Is he a man who always keeps his promises? I came back to the Midwest determined to leave the lying and intrigue behind me. Instead, I walked right into a situation with a man like Wally. A man who lives in the shadows like I used to. What am I doing with him?

He rubs a hand up and down my back, and I have to breathe deeply to stop myself from shivering with how good it feels to have him comfort me. I promised myself I'd stay out of trouble after what happened in the desert. I'm afraid letting Wally near is not only breaking my promise to myself, it's ripping the thing up and throwing it into the fire.

"Angel?"

And why does his pet name make my tummy turn to mush? "I'm no angel."

"You're my angel."

"Corny."

"How's this for corny?" he whispers before his lips meet mine. His eyes are open as he studies my reaction to our lips meeting. When I don't protest, he nibbles my bottom lip before his tongue peeks out to lick. "I knew your lips would be soft."

I've been accused of a lot of things but soft isn't one of them. I bare my teeth before biting his bottom lip. He groans and all signs of softness are gone when his lips slam against mine. I gasp and his tongue sneaks into my mouth to duel with mine.

I can't thread my hands through his hair – it's too short – so I scratch my nails on his scalp. He moans into my mouth and his arms tighten around me.

"I think they're making out," Barney whisper-shouts.

"Pay up, suckers," Sid shouts.

Wally grunts before ending our kiss. "My brothers are assholes."

"Hey!" Pops yells. "I didn't say anything. I was just checking if I need to hire industrial cleaners to mop up blood."

"Blood? I think you mean—" I hear the sound of a slap and Barney's words cut off.

"We're leaving," Pops says.

Wally takes a deep breath, and I can feel his chest move since I'm standing in his arms. In his arms? What the hell am I doing?

Will I never learn my lesson? I shove at his shoulders, but he doesn't loosen his arms one tiny bit.

"No, you're not retreating from me. I won't allow it."

I roll my eyes. "Allow it? Don't try me, Mr. Bossy."

He winks. "Oh, I'll try you all right, Angel."

I'm not responding to his corniness. I latch onto an excuse to escape instead. "I need to return the dogs to Hailey and Aiden."

"I'll give you some time, but our relationship has changed," Wally declares and lets his arms drop.

I flick him a wave as I leave because I have no response. I'm afraid he's right, though. No, not afraid. Freaking terrified is more like it.

Chapter 13

Why do spies never use capitalization? They like to stay low-key.

"Hey, Angel," Wally greets as I enter the auditorium with Hailey. I give him a two-fingered wave and keep on moving.

Hailey notices the interaction. Of course, she does. She is a PI after all. She may be specialized in finding cheating spouses, but she's got situational awareness down pat. Her uncles have trained her well. Damn them.

"What's going on? I heard you and Uncle Wally were all snuggly last night."

I sigh. This group and their meddling in each other's business. I couldn't have chosen a different PI firm to work in? Maybe found a place I can be anonymous? Instead, I walked into a freaking *Cheers* episode. I don't want everyone to know my name. I want to be left alone.

I ignore Hailey as I notice Suzie waving to us from a front-row near the podium. She's standing between two older couples. Older? Snort. They're probably not much older than me. Crap. Am I middle-aged now? I didn't approve this change in status.

We join Suzie and she introduces us. "On my right side are my parents, Sharon and Philip."

I shake his hand. "Mr. and Mrs. Langley, it's nice to meet you."

"Call me Sharon," the woman shouts before pulling me into her arms. "You're a tall one, aren't you?"

I disengage myself from the woman as quickly as I can without it being awkward. "And you're the short one."

She guffaws. "I like this one," she tells her daughter. "Who does she belong to?"

I scowl. I belong to no one. But before I have a chance to tell her how sexist and outdated her statement is, Susie responds, "Wally."

Sharon's eyes widen. "Wally?" She licks her lips. "He is one fine specimen of manhood. Well done."

Okay then. I guess Suzie came by her craziness the old-fashioned way – she inherited it.

"We're not together," I claim.

Suzie snorts. "You were caught canoodling at McGraw's last night."

"Canoodling?"

"You know…" She wraps her arms around herself and makes kissing sounds.

Sharon claps. "Wonderful. More babies."

"How old do you think I am? You want more babies talk to Phoebe or Hailey. Phoebe's already pregnant, so I guess Hailey is the one to talk to."

"Phoebe's pregnant!" She shrieks and rushes off to tackle the poor woman. Ryker spots her coming and stands in front of his wife and glares down at Sharon who is undeterred. She shoves past him and throws her arms around Phoebe.

Suzie throws a hand in the air like she's won some victory. Then, she points to Barney. "You owe me!"

"Calm down, Suzie," the man standing next to her barks.

Since no one's introducing us, I stick out my hand. "Hi, I'm Chrissie. I work with Hailey and Phoebe."

"And she's Wally's paramour," Suzie sings.

I drop my hand and frown at her. "What is it with you and the old-fashioned word usage today? And maybe you should research your vocabulary more. Paramour usually refers to the illicit partner of a married person. I'm not married." I was engaged, but we never actually said our vows because the man turned out to not be who I thought he was.

She waves away my argument. "Whatever. Did anyone bring a fire extinguisher because Wally's smoldering gazes at you could start this auditorium on fire? Ay caramba!"

I glance over my shoulder to find Wally is indeed staring at me with heat in his eyes. I narrow my eyes at him, and he smirks.

I return my attention to the couple. Let's try this again. I stick out my hand. "You must be Grayson's parents. It's nice to meet you."

"Norman," his dad says while shaking my hand. "The woman next to me crying is my wife, Armela."

She slaps him. "I'm not crying yet," she claims despite the tears welling in her eyes.

Norman rolls his eyes and leans close to whisper. "She will be, though. You can bet on it."

What is with these people and betting?

"I will cry if I want to. Our boy is graduating from college today, he's married and has a child on the way. And he's happy. A year ago, we thought Grayson would never come out from under the burden of his guilt, so excuse me if I cry a little," Armela says and promptly bursts into tears.

Norman grunts before hauling her into his arms. Suzie piles on to make it a group hug.

I look away to find Suzie's mom, Sharon, and Barney strolling my way. "What did the toaster say to the slice of bread?" Sharon asks him with a waggle of her eyebrows. "I want you inside me."

Barney chuckles before launching into a joke himself. "What do a penis and a Rubik's Cube have in common? The more you play with it, the harder it gets."

He lifts his hand and Sharon slaps it.

"Mom," Suzie whines.

"What? We're all adults here."

Suzie doesn't have a chance to respond before Faith and Max arrive, and Faith asks, "What did we miss?" Judging by her shortness of breath, messed up hair, and bright red cheeks, I don't need to ask why they're late.

"Suzie's mom is completely crazy. She's having a dirty joke contest with Barney."

Max kisses my hair. "You okay, darling?"

"Nothing to report," I tell him. He stares at me for a second, and I stare right back. After a minute, he grunts and moves along to where Wally is standing with Lenny and Sid.

Hailey waves Faith and me over from where she's sitting with Aiden. Next to them are Phoebe and Ryker. Ryker is fussing over Phoebe.

"Stop it. I'm perfectly fine," Phoebe hisses at Ryker as Faith and I join them.

"These seats are hard. I don't want you getting a sore back." Ryker holds up a portable seat cushion.

"I'm more concerned about needing the restroom during the ceremony." Phoebe's skin does have a greenish tint to it.

"I've got you covered." He holds up a barf bag.

She slaps the thing down. "Are you crazy?" She hisses. "I'm not puking into a bag in an auditorium filled with thousands of people."

Ryker shrugs. "No problem. The closest restroom is twenty-five meters away."

She throws her hands in the air. "I don't know how to respond to you right now."

Faith sits next to her, and I search for another available seat. Wally motions to the empty spot next to him. Yeah, right. I guess I'm sitting next to Suzie and her crazy family.

The lights flicker and it's time for the ceremony to begin. When I realize how many folded chairs are set up for the graduates, I groan. This ceremony is going to last all day. I don't blame Ryker for being worried about Phoebe's comfort. My behind is already sore, and we've barely begun.

My phone vibrates in my pocket. Oh great. A text from Wally.

You can ignore me all you want today, but it doesn't change a thing. This is happening.

I can't resist responding. I never was a cautious person as evidenced by my former profession.

This? Whatever do you mean?

I swallow my laughter. I'm having too much fun egging him on.

Don't poke the dragon.

He's asking for it now.

**Scratches head* I thought you were the one to do the poking.*

I tilt my head to hide the smile on my face.

Angel, when the time is right, I'll be glad to show you how hard I can poke.

Geez. Is it hot in here all of sudden?

Suzie slaps my hand. "Put your phone away. Grayson's almost up."

I stow my phone and watch as Grayson steps up to the podium. He glances in our direction and Suzie waves with two hands at him and ends up smacking me in the face. Grayson shakes his head at her, but his smile stretches from ear to ear. Easy for him to smile. He isn't the one with the sore nose. For being oblivious, Suzie has pretty good aim.

"Grayson Eliot Neil," is announced and everyone in our row jumps to their feet to scream and shout.

"HONK!!!"

I cover my ears at the sound of an air horn. What the hell? I glance at Suzie and spot she's ready to press the button again. I snatch it out of her hands. "No!"

"But—"

"No. Sit down. He's already off the stage."

It's true. Grayson is now on the side of the stage where he's posing for pictures for Hailey.

Suzie harrumphs and flops down in her seat. "Fine. But I want the record to show you're no fun."

I nod. "Duly noted."

I disconnect the horn from the gas and hand it back to Suzie. She pouts but puts the parts into her bag for safekeeping. Knowing her, we haven't seen the last of the air horn.

Another half an hour passes before all the students have walked across the stage. By the time they announce the ceremony is finished, my butt is sore, and my back is aching. I wonder how Phoebe is fairing, but when I search the crowd for her, she's nowhere to be found. Knowing Ryker, he ushered her out after Grayson was finished.

"Now what?"

"Now, it's time to par-tee!" Suzie waves her hands in the air, and I duck before she can smack me again. The woman's hands should be classified as dangerous weapons.

I have no intention of going to McGraw's Pub for Grayson's graduation party. I need to put some distance between me and a certain male someone. I slip away but when I round the corner to the parking garage, Wally is there waiting on me.

"Son of a bitch," I mutter before I can stop myself.

"You're not trying to sneak off, are you?"

"Nope. I need to check on Gray. She's never been alone for more than a few hours."

I'm not lying. I've only had the little furball for a few days, and I've been going home to check on her a few times a day. It's probably not necessary, but Gray gives the best cuddles.

Wally studies me for a few seconds before nodding. "I'll give you this play, but you can't avoid me forever."

I widen my eyes and feign innocence. "I'm not playing."

He chuckles. "You're full of crap, Angel, but I'm not worried. I'll wear you down eventually."

Which is what I'm afraid of. I don't tell him I'm afraid, though. I know better than to tease a predator with the smell of blood. Instead, I wave as if his presence has zero effect on me. "See ya."

"You certainly will, Angel. You certainly will."

I need to use all of my training to stop myself from running away from Wally.

Chapter 14

Two spies got caught using a book code to communicate. Clearly, they weren't on the same page.

I WAKE WITH A start when I hear the distinctive sound of a beep from my alarm system. It's not an alarm. An alarm is loud and would inform an intruder his presence has been detected. I don't want an intruder to know I'm aware he's in the house and I'm coming after him.

I slip out of the bed and grab my 9 mm from where it's laying on top of my nightstand. I creep as quietly as I can to my bedroom door. The door stands open since a closed door is a false sense of security. I plaster myself to the back of the wall next to the door and count to five before sticking my head in the hallway to survey the situation.

A shadow moves across the mouth of the hallway in the direction of my kitchen. I pursue the shadow making sure to keep my footfalls quiet. I don't want whoever it is to be aware of me yet. First, I want to find out who it is and what they want.

I observe as the person opens and closes drawers in my kitchen. I estimate the person is at least a few inches taller than six feet. Add in the broad shoulders and flat chest, and It's clear I'm dealing with a male intruder.

I have no idea what this man is doing. A common thief wouldn't bother searching through my kitchen drawers. Of course, a common thief wouldn't be able to disable my alarm system either. Although, he doesn't know everything as the subtle flash of a red light on the alarm panel indicates the police have been alerted to the break-in.

If I want to interrogate this man before the police arrive, I need to make my move soon. I clear my throat. "Ahem. Is there something, in particular, you're searching for? Maybe I can help you."

The man turns to me and raises his weapon. Mine is already aimed at him. He backs away toward the patio door. I wave my weapon at him. "Tsk. Tsk. I think we need to have a conversation about why you didn't knock when you came to visit me tonight."

He cocks his weapon in silent challenge. Two can play at this game. I feel behind me for the light switch. Flipping on the lights will ruin both of our night visions, but I'll have the advantage since I'll know it's happening.

I close my eyes and hit the switch. All the lights in the kitchen and dining area come on in full force. I blink my eyes, but the man is already rushing through the sliding door. Shit.

I rush after him and jump off of the deck to tackle him. I grab for him, but I miss his arm by mere inches. I roll to my feet and charge after him. He has the advantage, though, as my feet are bare, and I'm wearing a t-shirt and pajama pants. I never thought I'd miss a sports bra, but I do now.

I push through the pain of the cold wet ground on my feet and the discomfort of my boobs flapping all over the place and chase the intruder as he sprints through several backyards before ending on the street. He straddles a bike and zooms off into the night.

I stand in the middle of the street with my weapon aimed at the bike. I don't shoot, though. I have no authority to shoot a man in the back who's running away from me. I whirl around when I hear a vehicle flying toward me at high speed. It screeches to a halt in front of me and Wally jumps out.

I drop my weapon. "Black Kawasaki motorcycle, license plate ends in zero, five, one."

Wally doesn't question me. He types the information in his phone.

"Aren't you going after him?" I ask between gasps of breath.

"My brothers are on the case. I need to get you inside."

I wave away his concern. "I'm fine. Nothing a hot bath and cold whisky can't handle."

He ignores me to grasp my arm and lead me to his truck. I don't protest. Now the adrenaline is leaking out of me, I'm feeling the cold. He doesn't say anything as he drives the half block to my house.

"Wait here," he orders after parking in my driveaway.

I don't bother saying anything. I'm going to do whatever I want anyway. I follow him into my house, and we clear it before locking my patio door and re-engaging the alarm system.

"Sit. Let me inspect your feet."

"They're fine. A bit cold but I'm not bleeding all over the place, so I didn't break the skin."

He growls. "Sit down before I make you."

I eye him for a moment. I give myself a seventy-five percent chance of taking him on a normal day. But today, I'm sitting down because I don't have a chance. He's vibrating with anger, and I'm suffering from exposure to the cold.

I plop onto a chair and Wally kneels in front of me. He lifts my right foot and inspects it before setting it down to check out the other foot. "Your feet are blue with the cold," he complains as his thumb digs into my arch.

I cough to hide my moan. "This is what happens when you go for a jog without shoes in Wisconsin in December."

He scowls. "Why the hell did you chase him without any shoes on?" His gaze travels from my feet up my body. "For fuck's sake, you're wearing a t-shirt."

"I wasn't wasting time getting dressed after I heard the alarm go off."

I glance down and notice my nipples are hard and pointing toward Wally whose eyes are trained on them. I cross my arms over my chest to hide my body's reaction to the cold. Yes, cold. My nipples aren't tingling because he's staring at them with heat in his eyes.

Wally clears his throat and stands. "Get in the bath. I'll pour you a whisky."

"You can leave now," I say as I head toward my bathroom. "I'm good."

"Get warm first and then we'll discuss it."

I'm too cold for a fight. I'll stock up my reserves in the bath and then I'll be ready for a fight with Mr. Bossy.

I'm laying in the bath with my eyes closed when I hear the door creak open. I force one eye open to find Wally standing in the doorway.

"I talked to Aiden. You can give your statement at the police station tomorrow."

I figured as much. Having a police detective as an asset is handy. No, not an asset. A friend, Chrissie. You don't have assets anymore, remember? You're out. Except the intruder seems to think otherwise because he was clearly no burglar.

Wally steps into the bathroom, keeping his eyes diverted. Huh. Who would have thought he can be a gentleman?

"It's safe. The bubbles are covering all my assets."

He sets a glass of whisky on the edge of the tub. "Take your time. I'll be in the living room."

"Are you running scared?" I smirk. Wally scared. This is precious.

"No," he claims before adjusting his pants. My gaze zeroes in on his pants. His extremely tight pants. Oh.

Since I'm not ready to unwrap the hard package he's carrying, I pick up the whiskey and take a sip. "I'll be out in a few minutes."

"Take your time," he repeats before backing up and practically fleeing the room.

I sit in the bath until the water turns cold. Then, I rinse off in the shower before dressing in a pair of fuzzy pajamas and a fluffy robe. I need the layers to armor myself for the fight I know is coming with Wally.

As soon as I enter the living room, Wally switches off the television and gives me his attention.

"Do you know who the intruder was?"

I walk to the kitchen to pour myself another whiskey. I shake the bottle at him in a silent question. He nods and I bring the bottle into the living room and hand it to him.

I sit in the armchair and sip at my whisky before answering him. "No. He was dressed completely in black and wearing a balaclava. I estimate him to be about six-foot-three. No other distinctive characteristics were visible."

"My brothers lost him."

I figured as much. He wouldn't be sitting in my living room if the man had been found.

"I'm staying here until he's found."

I knew this was coming. "No, you're not. I'm perfectly safe."

"Do I need to remind you of the man who broke in here less than an hour ago?" he snaps.

"The alarm alerted me of his presence. I was never in any danger."

"You wouldn't have been in any danger at all if you hadn't chased him out of your house and down the street while you were practically naked."

"I admit I should have put my shoes on before slipping out of my bedroom, but I'm not wasting time getting changed before confronting an intruder."

"Confronting?" he grumbles.

"Dude, I am who I am. I've been trained with the best. I'm not going to hide in my closet. It's not me."

"Which is why I'm staying here until whatever's happening is resolved."

Not if I can help it, he won't. "We don't know the guy was after me. It could be some random burglar."

"Don't insult my intelligence with your bullshit." He pauses before proposing, "I'll sleep on the couch."

Not happening. "In your bed in your own home is where you'll sleep."

"Fine. I'll sleep in my car in your driveway."

Great. The neighbors are going to think I have a stalker. "The old lady across the street will call the police before you can fall asleep."

He smirks. "I guess I'll have to sleep on your couch then."

I down my whiskey and it burns my esophagus, but I don't let it show. I slam the glass down on the coffee table and stand. "Fine. I expect you to be gone by morning."

I don't wait for him to respond before marching to my bedroom and slamming the door closed. I don't expect sleep will be easy tonight.

Chapter 15

What does a spy do when they go to bed? They go under cover.

WALLY

Chrissie said she wanted me gone by morning, but I didn't agree to leave. No way am I leaving her alone when her home was breached last night. Plus, needing security is the perfect excuse to wear her down and get her used to me being around since I plan to be around for a long time. It's a win-win situation.

I flip the bacon in the pan, and it sizzles. I hear Chrissie come up behind me. I don't need to look to know she's there.

"You sleep well, Angel?"

She grunts. "Why are you still here? I told you to be gone by morning."

I pour her a cup of coffee and spin around to hand it to her. She glares at me before accepting the mug.

I wait until she's had a few sips before asking, "Better?"

"I'll be better when you leave. Which is happening when?"

I return my focus to the bacon. I place the strips on a plate before carrying it to the dining room table, which I've already set with plates and glasses of orange juice.

"I didn't have any orange juice in my refrigerator. Or bacon for that matter," Chrissie complains.

I kiss her forehead. "Delivery from Lenny."

She groans. "Great. Now all your brothers will be talking about how we had sex last night."

"They better not. I won't stand for it."

She snorts. "Please. As if you can stop them."

I can and I will. "Eat your bacon," I order as I remove a tray of pancakes from the oven.

"Pancakes, too? I would have been fine with the bacon."

"And you would have been hungry an hour later."

"Yes, Mom."

"Smartass," I kiss her hair as I pass her and sit across from her. "You need your energy. Aiden is expecting you at the police station in an hour."

She nods and piles food onto her plate. I like how she doesn't argue about every damn thing like other women. Chrissie picks her battles.

Forty-five minutes later, she steps into the living room having changed into a pair of jeans and a sweater for her trip to the police station. She halts when she spots me standing at the front door.

"You still here?"

Where else would I be? "Come on, Angel. I'll drop you at the station."

"Fine." She gives in because she doesn't realize I'm not going to leave after I drop her off.

"You going to be okay by yourself?" I ask when I pull up in front of the police station.

"This isn't my first rodeo." She opens her door, but I stop her with a hand on her arm.

"I know it isn't. I didn't ask about your experience. I asked if you're okay."

Her eyes warm and I know I've hit my target. Chrissie's tough as hell, but she hasn't had anyone to have her back for a long time. I assume since her parents died, and her asshole family blamed her for their deaths. Things are changing starting now. I'm going to be the man who has her six, whether it's on the job or in private. She will learn she can count on me.

"I'm fine," she says and then hops out of the truck before I can respond.

I chuckle. Doesn't she realize her running is making me chase her? And I do love a good chase. I park the car in a spot where I can keep an eye on the entrance to the police station. While she's inside, I do some research on crime in her area.

I'm certain her situation is unique, but I want to cover all my bases. It's as I suspected. Burglaries in her area are rare and none of the breached houses had a security system. Plus, all of the owners were on vacation when their houses were burglarized.

I hold my finger over my boss's contact information. I know if I call him, he'll tell me everything I want to know about Chrissie. I already questioned him before, but he denied any knowledge of a Christina Lundberg. But now that I know for certain Chrissie worked for the agency, he won't be able to lie to me again. In the end, I put my phone away. I have a feeling if I break my promise to Chrissie to stop digging around in her past, she'll never forgive me.

When I spot Chrissie exiting the building an hour later, I switch on the truck engine and drive to the entrance. She shakes her head, but she doesn't hesitate to open the door and climb in.

"How come I'm not surprised to find you here?"

I don't bother answering her. I drive toward the surprise I've arranged for today.

"Where are you going? This isn't the way to my house. Are you kidnapping me? Because you kind of suck at it. The police station has numerous cameras – all of which recorded your vehicle. And Aiden knows you dropped me off. Plus, I have my phone and I'm armed."

"I'm not kidnapping you, but thanks for the tips in case I change my mind."

"Like you need tips," she mutters.

We both know I've kidnapped people in my life. Although, I don't really consider my actions as kidnapping. Not when they were necessary to stop the mass murder of innocent civilians.

I park in front of an old warehouse fifteen minutes later.

"If you brought me here to interrogate me, you're wasting your time."

I flip the middle console up and unhook her seatbelt before hauling Chrissie into my lap. She has her weapon out and aimed at my forehead before I can get her settled.

"Thanks for the reminder," I tell her while acting unconcerned about having a weapon aimed at my skull. I am unconcerned since the safety is still engaged. "We need to put our weapons in my gun safe before we go inside."

"You need to not haul me around like I'm a ragdoll."

I can tell by the flush of her cheeks and the increase of her breathing, she likes being exactly where she is. Taking my life into my own hands, I rub my nose against hers. "Okay, Angel. If you don't want me to haul you around, I won't." Notice I didn't say I won't haul her around. I'm no dummy.

She stares at me for a few seconds before grunting and holstering her weapon. She tries to climb off my lap as well, but my fingers dig into her hips to keep her right where she is.

"I like you here," I tell her.

"Do I have to explain once again how we're not in a relationship?"

I rub my nose against her jaw, and I notice goosebumps break out on her skin. I angle my head to hide my grin at her reaction.

"We are, Angel. We are. Fight it all you want. I don't care. I am not a man to give up when he's seen what he wants."

"What are we doing here?" she asks instead of responding to my declaration. Typical diversion tactic and completely expected.

"I've got a surprise for you."

"Does it involve shooting holes in you?"

I open my door and pick her up off my lap before setting her on the ground next to the truck. "How do you feel about parkour?"

She shrugs. "Never done it before."

"This place has a parkour course developed using military obstacle course techniques."

Her eyes light up. I knew she'd like this. Chrissie likes to train and keep her body fit and she's competitive as hell. This parkour course is the perfect way for her to rid her body of the anxiety caused by last night's intruder.

She rubs her hands together. "It sounds like it's time to kick some old man ass." She can try.

We secure our weapons in my gun safe before I grasp her hand and lead her to the entrance of the facility. I booked the place for an hour for private use. I don't want any civilians to know what an old man is capable of and rouse their suspicions.

Chrissie bounces on her toes as she scans the room with its various obstacles we need to climb, vault, jump to, and crawl through.

"What do I win when I kick your ass, old man?"

The way her eyes are sparkling in anticipation she can have just about anything from me.

"What do you want?"

She taps her chin as she thinks about it. "You can clean my house." I saw how clean she keeps her place. This will not be a hardship. "While wearing a maid's uniform, including feather duster."

I chuckle. "All right. And if I win, we're going out on a date." Another date to be exact, but I'm not stupid. I know better than to mention our first date.

She hesitates a moment before sticking her hand out. "Doesn't matter what your prize is because I'm going to kick your ass."

I squeeze her hand. I have no qualms about being bested by a woman, but I will win this bet, because Chrissie and I are going out on another date, come hell or high water.

Chapter 16

Why don't spies meet at bars? The beer is tapped.

"You totally cheated, dude," I complain as Wally leads me into McGraw's Pub on Saturday evening. My body tingles at the feel of his hand pressing into my lower back, which serves to irritate me more. I speed up, but Wally keeps right up with me.

"How did I cheat?" I can hear the smile in his voice. The cheating jerk.

"You can't tell someone you can't wait to taste every inch of her naked body when she's about to jump from an obstacle."

I was gearing up to sprint from one block to the next when Wally leaned over and said those exact words into my ear. Every nerve ending in my body engaged sending a full body shiver through me. I tripped and ended up having to start the obstacle over.

"You got me back when you said my manhood couldn't possibly be as big as my ego."

It was a totally lame response, and Wally didn't fall for it, so it doesn't count.

"Fat lot of good it did me."

My feet freeze on the threshold to the pub. I don't want to go in there with Wally like we're a couple.

"We're not in a relationship," I remind him. I don't know who I'm reminding – him or me.

He smirks. "Maybe if you lie to yourself about us another hundred times, you'll actually start believing it."

His hand travels from my lower back to my shoulder and he pulls me close before opening the door. My stomach warms and my body leans toward him before my head catches on and I yank out of his grasp, but he snatches my hand before I can get too far.

"Pay up!" Sid shouts before we've even entered the bar.

I whirl around and stomp out of the bar. I have no interest in being the topic of discussion of his brothers. Wally follows me. Of course, he does. "I'm not reneging on the bet. We can eat dinner together somewhere else some other time."

He chuckles. "This isn't our date. This is merely dinner."

"Fine. I'll go home then. I can eat there."

He shrugs. "We can order take-out."

"No, Mr. Bossy, *I* can order take-out. *You* can go home."

"No." He shakes his head. "We agreed I'd stay at your house until the intruder was found."

I poke him in the chest and nearly break my finger. What the hell is this man doing for an exercise regime? Shouldn't he be sporting a beer belly at his age?

"*We* didn't agree to anything. You railroaded me into feeling sorry for you because I didn't want you sleeping in your truck during a Wisconsin winter."

He cups my face with his hand. "Come on, Angel. I can't bear the thought of you in danger."

I lean back so he has to drop his hands because my body likes the feel of his hands on my body entirely too much. Stupid, slutty body with a malfunctioning memory.

"I can handle myself."

"I know, but I don't want you to have to."

Damnit. It's a good answer. I can't let his words sway me, though. I've been down this road before – thinking I can trust a man – it only leads to betrayal and destruction. Two of my least favorite things in the world. I'll pass.

Wally frowns for a moment. "How about this? You have dinner with me tonight here at McGraw's and I won't insist on staying with you."

I narrow my eyes on him. There's no doubt in my mind. He's up to something. "And you won't park your truck in my driveaway and keep vigil all night?"

"I won't park in your driveaway."

"Or in my street," I tack on.

He sighs. "Fine. I won't park in your street all night either. You satisfied?"

I'm not completely certain he didn't trick me somehow, but I nod anyway. "Let's get this over with."

He places his hand on my lower back and opens the door again. This time when we enter it's Barney who shouts, "Pay up!"

I smirk before pretending to glance behind me. "Hi, Valerie! I didn't know you were coming here tonight."

Barney's eyes widen before he climbs to his feet and rushes toward the hallway. I don't bother trying to disguise my evil laugh as I watch him disappear around the corner.

"You're mean," Wally whispers into my ear.

"He asked for it."

He grasps my hand and leads me to an empty booth in the back. I drag my feet. "Where are you going? Your table is the other way." I point to the table the brothers always sit at.

"I want to have dinner with you, not my brothers."

I throw my hands in the air. "Then, why did you bring me here?"

"Like I don't know you would have thrown a fit if I went anywhere else."

I glare at him. I hate how he's right. To his credit, he doesn't smirk. This time.

Pops arrives at our table. "Ignore the idiot brothers, darling," he tells me before kissing my forehead.

Wally growls. "Brother."

Pops winks at me before looking over at Wally, fake confusion on his face. "What is it?"

Wally's eyes narrow. "You know what."

"The brothers were right. This is fun."

Wally starts to stand but Pops places a hand on his shoulder to keep him down. "I'm playing with you. Calm down."

"How would you feel if I kissed Faith?" Wally grumbles.

Pops crosses his arms over his chest. "Completely different situation. Faith's my wife."

"Not yet, she isn't."

I'm done with them talking like I'm not here. "She already picked out the dress and the date is set. She's as good as his wife."

Pops squeezes my shoulder. "Thanks for going with her to help her."

"I didn't help. I have no idea how to help a woman pick out a wedding dress. You need help picking out the right handgun, I'm your girl. Dresses? No way."

"I think we're good on handguns. What can I get you to drink?"

After we order a couple of beers from Suzie's brewery and some burgers, Pops saunters off. Wally reaches for my hand across the table. I frown at him and cross my arms over my chest.

"What are you doing? This isn't a date."

"Angel, anytime you're near I want to be touching you."

Sigh. "Come on, Wally. You're a fifty-nine-year-old man who's never been in a relationship. You can't possibly want one now with me."

"We've already talked about this, but I'll tell you this until I'm blue in the face. I'm a man who knows exactly what he wants, and I want a relationship with you."

Ugh. There's no arguing with crazy. Distraction is my only option. "You want to play a game of pool while we wait for our food?" I don't wait for him to reply before standing and marching to the pool tables.

I can hear him chuckling behind me as he follows me. Whatever.

In less than a minute, I realize playing pool with Wally was a bad idea – a very bad idea. Every time he saunters past me, he makes sure to brush my hip with his hand. And whenever I look up from my shot, he's there staring at me with heat in his eyes.

"Psst," Barney motions to me.

This ought to be good. I rest my pool cue against the wall and join Barney while Wally takes his shot.

"What?"

"Shh… not so loud."

It's Saturday night and the bar is hopping. I could shout and Wally wouldn't hear me.

"What is it?" I say in a slightly lower voice. I'm not going to whisper like an idiot. I can tell Wally's already suspicious as it is.

"Can you get Wally to go to the restroom?"

Ah, prank time has arrived. "And how do you propose I manage that?"

"You can offer him an incentive." He waggles his eyebrows.

"You're an idiot," I tell him.

I admit I am curious what the prank is, though. We finish our game, which Wally wins. Grrr… And I announce I need the restroom.

"I'll escort you," Wally says as I suspected he would.

"I'm perfectly safe here, Mr. Bossy."

"Maybe I'm being a gentleman."

He places a hand on my lower back – ugh! Why do I like his hand there this much? – and leads me down the hallway to the restrooms. I enter the ladies' room but walk right back out when I hear his footsteps heading toward the men's room.

Sid, Barney, and Lenny are already waiting in the hallway. Yep. It's definitely prank time. I watch as Wally opens the men's room door, and an air horn sounds off. "HONK!!!"

"Did you steal Suzie's air horn?" I ask Barney.

"Grayson said she had to throw it away. It would have been a waste."

Wally marches out of the restroom and snarls at Barney, "What the hell did I do to you?"

Although the brothers love to prank each other, there's usually a reason for the prank. Barney shrugs, and Wally turns on me.

"And you? You helped them lure me to the men's room."

I cross my arms over my chest. "Dude, what did you expect? You cheated at parkour." I start to bring out how he stuck his nose in my business, but I stop myself. I need to learn to stop bringing up old shit, especially since he's apologized and promised to stop digging around in my past.

Wally shakes his head before palming my neck and dragging me to him. His lips meet mine before I realize what's happening. From far away, I hear someone say, "I'm totally winning this bet." But right now, with Wally's lips on mine and his tongue exploring my mouth, I could care less about the brothers and their stupid bets.

Oh boy. If those thoughts don't spell trouble, I don't know what does.

Chapter 17

What's it called when spies perform Hamlet?
Thespionage.

"*You Cheat, We Eat*, how may I help you?" I barely manage to ask without yawning. It's Monday morning, and I didn't get much sleep last night or the night before for that matter. Who knew sexual frustration causes insomnia?

Wally dropped me off at my house on Saturday night after an evening spent having way more fun than I thought possible at a bar without getting into a gunfight, kissed me thoroughly in his truck, and then escorted me to the door and left me home alone. When I asked why he didn't come in and finish what he started in his truck, he told me he was being a gentleman. Gentleman? I never asked him to be a gentleman.

"I'd like to order a hamburger and fries, please," the voice on the other end of the phone says and jars me out of my reverie about Wally and the things he can do with his tongue.

My body warms as I imagine all the places I'd like to feel his tongue. Stop it, Chrissie! The man wants a relationship, and we don't do relationships, remember?

"Um, hello! Is anyone there?"

Oh crap. The caller. "Sorry. I think you've got the wrong number. We're a PI firm, not a restaurant."

"But the business is called *You Cheat, We Eat,* isn't it?"

"It is. It's a pun."

"It's not a pun. A pun is a joke exploiting the different possible meanings of a word or how there are words which sound alike but have different meanings."

Awesome. I'm getting schooled by someone who thinks a PI firm is a restaurant. "A play on words, then. The bottom line is we don't serve food. Have a lovely day." I hang up before she has a chance to respond and explain what a play on words is.

I square my shoulders before addressing the two women who think they snuck into the reception area while I was on the phone without me realizing it. When will they learn they can't sneak up on me?

"What can I do for the two of you?"

Hailey opens her mouth to respond, but I hold up a hand. "Let's wait for Suzie to arrive first, shall we?"

Suzie opens the door five seconds later, and Hailey's mouth gapes open. "How did you know?"

Because an elephant is quieter than Suzie stomping down the hallway. I cock an eyebrow. "How did you not know?"

"What did I miss?" Suzie asks as she plops into a chair next to Phoebe. "Hey, preggers sister."

Phoebe beams as she rubs her still flat belly.

"How is it you're still skinny and my belly is bigger than a basketball?" Suzie whines but there's a smile on her face as she too rubs her belly.

Hailey grunts. "Your sports references suck. Your belly is the size of a tennis ball at most."

I stand. "Where are you going?" Hailey shouts.

"To make myself a coffee. I have a feeling I'm going to need fortification for this conversation."

Ryker grunts. I stick my head inside his office. "Say please first."

"Black espresso, please."

"Coming right up!"

I normally hate making other people coffee. Do I look like a barista? But I'm not in a hurry to hear whatever the three stooges have to say.

"I swear my husband can speak in full sentences," Phoebe says in a loud voice ensuring Ryker can hear her.

"Only for you, Princess."

Phoebe swoons at Ryker's response. I finish making his espresso and bring it to him. I slam the cup down on his desk. "No nookie in the office when I'm here or I'll make you regret it."

He lifts his chin to signal his agreement. I nod and twirl around. I dawdle while making myself a coffee.

"Do you want one, Hailey?"

Before Hailey can respond, Phoebe moans. "It's not fair. You couldn't have bought a coffee machine before I got pregnant?"

"By my calculations, you were pregnant before I met you," I say in response.

"Who hired the know-it-all?" Phoebe grumps.

Hailey whips her hand into the air. "I did. And I'd love a cappuccino."

I make her coffee and then I'm out of excuses. I sit down behind my desk and wait for the interrogation to begin.

"You know what we want to know," Hailey says.

Yep. I do, but I'm not making it easy for them.

"Have you or have you not had sex with Wally?" Suzie demands.

Ryker's chair creaks before I hear his footfalls approach. "I'm out of here." He kisses Phoebe on the side of her head before hurrying out of the office.

I point at him. "Can I go with him?"

"No! This wouldn't be an intervention if the intervenee isn't here."

Hailey sighs at Suzie. "Intervenee isn't a word. Why did I bother buying you a dictionary if you're not going to use it?"

"And this isn't an intervention," Phoebe points out. "An intervention is when you're trying to persuade someone to stop doing an activity usually drugs or some other addictive behavior. We don't want Chrissie to stop doing Wally. We want Chrissie to jump his bones."

I'm surprised to hear Phoebe talking about sex this openly. She seems like a shy thing to me. But while her cheeks darken, she doesn't shy away from my gaze. The woman has a backbone. Good for her.

"Are we doing a lecture on the usage of the English language or are we going to grill Chrissie about her relationship with Wally?" Suzie asks.

I vote lecture on the English language despite English not being my strongest class in college. I speak the language, why do I need to spend hours discussing the grammar? Boring. I choose a lecture on chemistry and how to blow things up over English every day of the week and twice on Sunday.

"Well?" Hailey asks with a raised brow.

Oh, how cute. She thinks I'm going to make this easy for her. She has a lot to learn. I grin as I stare right back at her.

"Yikes!" She yips. "She's initiating a stare-down. Someone help me!" She covers her face with her hands. She forgets she's holding a coffee cup and ends up spilling coffee all over her shirt.

Phoebe giggles. "She got the Suzie klutzy gene."

"Hey now! I'm not a klutz."

Phoebe snorts at Suzie's denial. "Tell it to someone who didn't witness you knock yourself out."

My phone buzzes with a message and I read it while Suzie sputters her denial.

I'll pick you up at six.

Wally's really pushing it now. I don't care if I spent the entire weekend being sexually frustrated. He has no right to order me around. I should have never let him kiss me. Screw him and his soft lips and talented tongue.

Why?

I want to write who do you think you are, but I can guess his response to my question, and I don't want to hear his answer.

Ollie's birthday party tonight.

Oops. I forgot all about Ollie's birthday. Good thing I already bought his present last week.

I'll meet you at the bar.

I'll pick you up. Later.

I throw the phone down on my desk. The man is beyond frustrating.

"Ten bucks says those messages were from Wally," Suzie shouts.

"I'm not betting against it. Look at her face." Hailey points to me. "If you search frustrated with the male species in the dictionary, Chrissie's current expression will be there."

"I don't think there's a definition for frustrated with the male species in the dictionary," Suzie says.

"Now you know what's in the dictionary?"

Phoebe heaves herself to her feet. "Welp. If she's frustrated with Wally, she definitely hasn't had sex yet. Might as well get back to work." She pauses and gulps for air. "Excuse me," she barely manages to get out before rushing to the toilet. Mere seconds later, we can hear the sound of her throwing up.

Hailey makes a face. "If this is what it's like to be pregnant, I want no part of it."

Suzie bumps her shoulder. "You have to get pregnant so our children can grow up together. Oh." She claps and jumps up and down. "You can have a girl, I'll have a boy, and they'll fall in love."

"Your son is not taking advantage of my daughter," Hailey barks.

Suzie's eyes widen. "You're pregnant?" She wraps her arms around Hailey, and they fall to the ground.

I sigh before standing to help them untangle from each other. I pull Suzie to her feet, but Hailey waves my assistance away.

"Hailey's pregnant?" Phoebe shouts from the bathroom before the sound of her gagging can be heard again.

"Do you want to tell them or shall I?" I ask Hailey. She shrugs. "Hailey's not pregnant. She was drinking a coffee less than fifteen minutes ago, remember?"

Suzie's shoulders slump. "Oh yeah. Wait. Do you need me to have Grayson talk to Aiden about how to satisfy you? I don't mean to brag or anything, but Grayson is pretty good at the sexy times."

Hailey snarls at Suzie. "Aiden can run circles around Grayson in the bedroom."

Suzie's nose wrinkles. "If Aiden is running in the bedroom, I think he's doing it wrong."

Hailey's head drops. "Why do I have crazy friends? Why?"

"I'm not crazy," Phoebe shouts from the bathroom. "I may stay in here all day, though. Does Doordash deliver to toilets?"

"Thanks for proving my point Phoebe," Hailey shouts before retreating to her office.

Suzie scans the area as if wondering where everyone went. I decide to help her out. "In summary, Wally and I aren't together, Hailey isn't pregnant, and Phoebe's morning sickness is bad."

She taps the side of her nose. "Gotcha. See you guys tonight!"

Thanks for the reminder. For a minute there, I forgot all about Wally and the impending evening. How am I supposed to resist the guy when our friend groups are intertwined to the point of being family? Damn him and his delectable lips.

Chapter 18

In what part of a hospital do they spy on patients?
In the I.C.U.

I'M HURRYING TO GET dressed and out of the house when the doorbell rings at half-past five. I rush to the door putting on my shoes as I go but when I get a glimpse of who's standing on my front porch, I freeze. Son of a bitch.

Wally knocks again. "I know you're in there, Angel."

I eye the sliding door to the backyard. He'd never catch me if I snuck out the back. But my car's parked in the garage and it's a five-mile hike to the pub. Damnit. I thought leaving at 5:30 would give me plenty of time to avoid Mr. Bossy. Guess not.

I whip open the door. "What are you doing here?"

"I'm happy to see you, too, Angel," he says before kissing my forehead.

Ugh! Why do his forehead kisses make me want to melt into his arms? Arms I know will catch me. No. They won't catch me. Men can't be trusted, remember? The more time I spend around Wally, the more difficult I'm finding it to remember how deceitful men can be.

"You ready?"

His words startle me out of thoughts about whether Wally is to be trusted. "I'm driving myself."

"It's snowing, and your car doesn't have winter tires on it."

Seriously? Can he be more infuriating? "I was fine driving to work today."

"And today is the last time you're driving on summer times this winter."

Now, he went too far. "Stop pushing me around."

He wraps a hand around my neck to pull me near. "Then, start taking your safety seriously."

He doesn't give me a chance to answer before he melds his lips to mine. I clutch the lapels of his jacket to stay upright. Not because his kiss causes me to swoon – I'm not some romance novel heroine – but because he caught me off-guard, and I need to steady myself is all.

His kiss is all too brief. His eyes crinkle with his smile as he tells me, "That is how you greet your man."

I use my hold on him to shove him away. "You had to ruin it, didn't you?"

"Alarm your system, so we can leave."

"Alarm your system, so we can leave," I parrot as I alarm the stupid system.

"You're cute when I've got you all riled up."

"I'm not riled up." It's a lie. The man has the ability to cause my carefully constructed mask to fall into bits at my feet with a flick of his hand. It's terrifying.

I stop fighting because I'm not going to win this round. Besides, if Wally drives, then I can drink as much as I want.

I know better than to drink too much in this man's presence, but this is the reason I'm telling myself for why I'm letting him drive. It's not because I want to be around Wally as much as I can. It's not.

There's a sign on the door of McGraw's declaring the pub closed for a private celebration tonight when we arrive. Judging by the noise escaping the building, the private celebration is in full swing already.

"Who are all these people?" I ask as I scan the crowd.

Faith rushes in from the hallway and spots us. "Thank god, you're here."

"What do you need?"

She grabs my hand and drags me away. "I need someone to drink with. I thought having one teenager was difficult, but now I have a whole classroom of them."

Pops smiles as she approaches the bar. "Hey, sweetheart," he says before leaning over the counter to kiss her. And it's not some peck on the cheek either.

"Ugh! Gross! Not in front of the kid," Hailey shouts as she comes to stand next to me with Ollie.

Ollie hip checks Hailey. "Don't steal my line."

"They're my parents, too," Hailey says in a snotty voice.

Faith jerks away from Pops. "You better not be saying I'm your mom. I'm way too young to be your mom."

Hailey winks at me. "Gets her every time."

"Happy birthday, Ollie!" I tell him before handing him a present.

He doesn't hesitate to rip open the gift. His eyes widen when he removes the gift card for some tokens for some game. Honestly, I have no idea what it is. When Faith invited me to the party, I asked her what to buy Ollie and she suggested this. Guessing by his excitement, it was a good suggestion.

"Thanks, Chrissie! I'm going to show my friends," he declares before rushing off without a backward glance.

He nearly rams into Phoebe on his way. Ryker growls at him, and he pales before squeaking out the word sorry and running off again.

Phoebe joins us but her eyes are glued to the back room where Ollie and his friends are messing around. She rubs her tummy. "I don't know about this. Raising a teenager is going to be difficult."

Ryker draws her near. "Too late now, Princess."

"If it all goes wrong, I blame Faith. She's the one who convinced me I could be a parent."

Faith winks at her. "You'll be fine."

"I raised Hailey without any help, and she turned out fine," Pops declares.

"Better than fine, I'd say," Aiden says as he arrives and throws an arm around his wife.

Sid, Lenny, Barney, and Wally join us. "And you didn't raise her alone," Lenny declares.

Aiden frowns. "Don't expect me to be grateful to you for teaching her how to hotwire a car and circumvent an alarm system."

"Those are good skills to have." He frowns at my comment. "What? I'm not wrong."

Wally wraps his arm around me. "No, you're not."

I try to maneuver my way out from under his arm, but it's crowded, and I have no space to move without making a scene. I debate making a scene for a second before deciding on another tactic. My favorite tactic in fact – diversion.

"What did you get Ollie for his sixteenth birthday?" I ask Faith.

She glares at Pops who raises his hands in surrender. "He needs a car to be able to drive to school. I won't allow you to run yourself ragged being his chauffeur when your new job is stressful enough."

Faith sighs and the fight leaves her body. Pops is no dummy. He knows exactly what to say to calm her anger.

Phoebe groans. "They're making goo-goo eyes at each other like they're going to kiss again."

Suzie skids to a stop next to her and sways back and forth a few times before Grayson steadies her. "Who's kissing?" She rubs her hands together and bounces on her toes. "Please tell me it's Wally and Chrissie. Today's my day."

Grayson cups her elbow. "Stop bouncing. You're going to hurt the baby."

"I'm not going to hurt the baby. Stop being a baby."

"Real mature," he grumbles at her.

She goes to elbow him, but he shifts out of the way, and she flies backward. Before she can fall, he rescues her. "Be careful, klutzy girl."

"It's your fault. You're the one who moved."

Wally drops his arm from around my shoulders and tags my hand before dragging me to the hallway. Although – if I'm being honest, something I'm starting to hate to do – he doesn't have to work too hard to 'drag' me. He pushes me against the wall and boxes me in before cradling my face with his hands. I need to use all my willpower to stop myself from closing my eyes and leaning into him.

"Do you want children?"

I expected him to ravage my lips, not ask questions about children. And no, I'm not disappointed about missing out on the ravaging part.

"Whoa. Where did that question come from?"

"I want to give you everything your heart desires. Thus, do you want children?"

"Bossy, I'm too old to have children." He's fifty-nine and I'm forty-nine, the ship carrying the possibility of children has not only sailed, it's sunk to the bottom of the ocean.

"If you want them, we'll figure out a way. A surrogate if you want babies or we can adopt. If you want older children, then we can consider fostering with an eye to adoption."

I lean back until my head hits the wall. The impact doesn't cause me to wake up. I'm not asleep, and we're seriously having this conversation. Okay then.

"Where is this coming from? We're not even dating."

His nostrils flare as he insists, "Angel, we are dating." He places a finger on my lips to stop my protests. "Deny it all you want, but this is happening."

He brushes his finger back and forth over my lips and I can't resist opening my mouth. The second his finger slips in, I bite down on it. Not hard but enough to tease him. His eyes flare. What the hell am I doing? One second I'm telling him we're not dating and the next second I'm biting his finger in a tease. What is happening to me?

Wally rests his forehead against mine. "Angel, I know you have your reasons for fighting us being together. I understand. But I will prove to you I'm worth your time. Now, answer the question. Do you want children?"

I shake my head. "No, I don't. I know I'm supposed to want children because I'm a woman, but I don't. The world is a scary place and bringing an innocent baby into it is not something I'm prepared to do." Trust me, I've seen how horrible mankind can be.

"Then, we'll settle for spoiling the kids of our friends rotten."

"You helped Pops buy the car for Ollie, didn't you?"

He grins. "All of us did. We're his uncles. It's our right and privilege to spoil the kid. We spoiled Hailey and she turned out all right."

Hailey is pretty awesome.

"I'm done talking about children. I've got you in my arms right where I want you. I can think of a lot better things to do than talk."

I cock an eyebrow in challenge. "You can, can you?"

Hailey appears at the mouth of the hallway. "Come on, guys. You can make out later. Pops is giving Ollie his gift now. I can't wait to see his reaction."

Suzie shoves her. "Cheater! You know today's my day."

"All's fair in love and war," Hailey sings as she saunters off.

I duck under Wally's arm, but he catches my hand before I can make it far. "This will be continued later."

"Whatever." I try to sound flippant, but I actually can't wait for later.

Chapter 19

The U2 spy plane took many pictures during its military career. But it still hasn't found what it's looking for.

WALLY AND I ARE walking hand in hand toward his truck for him to drive me home when he freezes and begins swiveling his head left and right as he scans the area. I rest my hand on my pistol as I do the same, but I don't detect anyone or anything out of the ordinary until my glance falls upon the windshield of Wally's truck where a note flaps in the breeze.

I wrench my hand out of Wally's grip and march toward the truck. He grasps my shoulder in an effort to stop me, but I'm determined. We both know this is about me, and we both know he doesn't want me to read whatever's written on the note.

I snatch the note and he grumbles, "Fingerprints."

"Gloves," I say while I read the note.

I'm back, bitch.

No. This can't be true. It can't be *him.* I literally saw the building he was in blown to smithereens. He can't be alive. Except they never found his body and he always was a sneaky fucker. Hasn't he caused enough problems in my life? Forcing me to abandon my career and build a new life. And now he has to come here and ruin my new life, too? Asshole traitor.

Wally's arm wraps around me as he steers me toward the pub. I realize I'm shaking and lock it down. I can't fall apart right now. Not when there is a literal threat against me. Somewhere in the back of my mind I always knew the threat was real, but I didn't want to acknowledge it. Acknowledging it meant I would have to deal with it. Fat lot of good ignoring it did me.

The second we enter the pub the air electrifies. Pops herds the stragglers out of the place while Lenny, Barney, and Sid surround Wally and me as we head to the hallway leading to the office. When we arrive at the office, Wally tries to force me onto the sofa. I shove him off. I'm not some simpering woman in need of a rest. I'm a trained operative who needs to prepare for a mission. Except I'm no longer an operative. I'm a civilian.

I pace the room as Wally fills in his brothers about the note. Pops arrives a few minutes later, "The place is locked down."

Wally stands in front of me to stop my pacing. "It's time."

I don't need to ask what he means. I know exactly what he wants. "I can't. Classified."

Instead of responding, he removes his phone from his back pocket. He hits speaker before dialing a number and placing the phone on the desk in the middle of the office.

"Nelson, this better be good," a man answers the phone. Oh shit. I recognize the voice. Deputy Director Cruz.

"Director, I have a situation."

I hear the sound of sheets ruffling before the voice of the deputy director comes back on the line. "This line isn't secure."

"I'll keep in brief then," Wally says, and his eyes find mine before he says, "Christina Lindberg has just been threatened by a stalker."

Cruz swears under his breath for a few seconds. "I assume she's listening to this conversation."

"Affirmative."

"Chrissie, the rumors are true. He's alive."

Rumors? What rumors? Lexi didn't say anything about rumors. I bite my tongue to stop myself from spouting swear words like a sailor. This can't be happening.

"Who is he?" Wally asks.

"Chrissie can brief you."

"No, I can't. It's classified."

"Fuck, Chrissie," Cruz swears. "You've been disavowed and you're still maintaining the asshole's secrets? You want to stay alive? Trust Nelson. We never had this conversation," he says and hangs up.

Of course, we didn't. I loved my job with the agency but the cloak and dagger BS was my least favorite part. Apart from the whole being disavowed thing. Talk about a shitshow.

"You've been disavowed?" Wally grumbles. "What the hell happened?"

This is why you don't trust men. He heard the word disavow and now he thinks I'm a traitor.

"Pass. It's not like you're going to listen to my side of the story now anyway."

He growls before grasping my jaw. "You don't get to pass. Not when you're in danger, Angel. I warned you before. If you're in danger, I will shake every tree until every single secret you have comes crashing down."

"That was before you knew I was disavowed," I snarl.

His hand moves from grasping my jaw to palming my face. "Angel, I don't give a shit you've been disavowed."

I snort. "Yeah, right."

Those dark, green eyes soften. "Baby, I don't. I know you. You're the most loyal person in the world. If you've been disavowed, it's because you were betrayed." I flinch before I can stop myself. His hand drops to pull me into his arms. "Fuck, I get it now. This is why you protect your heart behind those walls."

Duh. You don't have walls as high as mine unless you've been hurt in the worst way possible.

Max clears his throat. "I hate to break this up, but we have a threat we need to deal with."

I shove Wally away, but he doesn't let me go far. He places his arm around my shoulders and squeezes. "It's time," he whispers.

I straighten my shoulders and lift my chin. I can do this. I survey the room and these men. Barney, Sid, Lenny, and Max aren't joking now. They're on high alert and they're here because they want to protect me. Not because of what my position can do for them, but because of the person I am.

I don't know how it happened, but somewhere along the way Wally's brothers became my brothers, and I trust them to keep my secret.

"This doesn't leave the room. Not even to the wives." I wait for Max and Sid to grunt in agreement before continuing.

"I don't think I need to tell you who my former employer was."

"No, darling," Max says and the others nod.

"Which is how I met my ex." I pause. His name is infamous in some circles. Circles I'm certain Wally is familiar with. I study his reaction as I say, "Flynn Price." His eyes narrow and it feels like the oxygen is being sucked out of the room. Judging by the expressions on the faces of the other men, they all know his name.

"I was in love with him." Wally growls, and I amend my statement, "I thought I loved him." The growl switches off, despite my words being a lie. I did love Flynn or the man I thought he was.

"You probably all know the story, you just didn't know who the woman in the story was. Flynn was selling secrets to the Russians. When our superiors got wind of his betrayal, he disappeared behind enemy lines in Syria. I, being an idiotic woman in love, didn't believe the rumors of him being a double agent. I was convinced Flynn would never betray his country." I snort. I was such an idiot.

"I disobeyed a direct order and went after him. I thought he needed saving." Like I said. Idiot. "I spent a month searching for him before I stepped foot in a hole in the wall in some no-name town in the Badia desert. He was laughing and drinking with two men known to be allied with the Russians as if nothing was wrong. I assumed he was working them, but when he saw me, his expression screamed panic like he was caught cheating red-handed. Then, I knew. I was wrong. I risked my career. My life. Everything for this man and he was a fucking traitor."

Wally reaches for me, but I step back. "No, let me finish this." He frowns, but his hand drops.

"I left, intent on finding my way back home, but I received a message from Flynn while I was waiting for my transport. He begged me to let him explain. Like the idiot I am, I agreed to meet him back at the bar. As I was crossing the street to the bar thirty minutes later, the place exploded."

"And you thought he was in there?" Lenny asks.

I shake my head. "Not thought. Knew. While I was surveying the area, I saw him enter the place not ten seconds before it blew."

"Good timing," Wally says.

"It had to be perfect timing for him to survive. I was across the street, and I was knocked on my ass." I turn around and flip my ponytail up to display the scar I sustained when glass from the bar was embedded in my skin.

Wally's fingers dance over the scar. "I felt the marred skin, but I was waiting for you to tell me what happened."

I roll my eyes. "Like you'll tell me how you sustained all your scars?"

"Angel, if you want to know, the stories are yours."

My eyes widen. I didn't expect his answer. He smiles. "You're not getting it yet, but you will. I'm going to give you everything, Angel." The smile disappears from his face. "But for now, we need to find Price and eliminate him."

"I'll get in touch with my contacts." I may be out, but I still have connections. "Now it's confirmed Flynn is alive, they'll want him."

"In the meantime, we need to make a roster to ensure you have round the clock protection." Wally stares at me as if waiting for me to fight him on this. I'm not stupid. I may have a skillset Hailey is envious of, but there's no way I can fight Flynn on my own.

Chapter 20

Why should you always bring your own cup to a spy's tea party? Their cups are always chipped.

WALLY

I pace the hallway as I wait at the bottom of the stairs to Max's apartment for him to come down. It's the middle of the night, but I messaged to ask him to meet me in the bar. As soon as I got Barney settled on guard duty outside of Chrissie's house, I came here.

Max opens the door, takes one look at me, and continues down the hallway to the bar. He pours two glasses of whiskey and sets one down in front of me. "I think you need this."

"What I need to do is hunt down Price."

"I feel you, brother, but going underground to find the jackass is the last thing you need right now."

I bare my teeth at him. "You have no idea."

He crosses his arms over his chest and cocks an eyebrow at me. "I don't? I don't know what it's like to feel like you're coming out of your skin because you think your woman *and* child are in danger?"

Shit. I scrub a hand down my face. Not too long ago Faith and Ollie were in danger. "It's not the same thing. Those gangs were in Saint Louis, not here in Milwaukee. We know Flynn, a traitor, is on Chrissie's doorstep waiting to attack."

Max slams a hand down on the bar. "Don't you dare! Don't you dare start claiming your dick is bigger than mine."

The door creaks open and Sid strolls inside. "Looks like I arrived right on time."

"You called Sid?"

"And me," Lenny calls out.

"What the hell?" I ask Max.

He spreads his arms wide. "I'm not an idiot. I know I can't take you on a good day. On a day when your woman has been threatened? I'm not convinced the three of us are enough to lock you down."

"I don't need to be locked down," I grit out.

Sid rubs his hands together. "This is going to be fun. It's worth missing out on a night sleeping with my woman in our bed."

Max grunts. "Nothing's worth missing out on a night spent with my woman in bed."

"I stand corrected. Almost worth missing out."

My nostrils flare. "This is not time for the Laurel and Hardy show."

Lenny slaps my shoulder. "Brother, we know. It's time for you to realize we have your back and won't let anything happen to your woman."

I shake off his hand. "I know. I also know she won't be truly safe until Price is dead." Captured is not good enough. Not for the sneaky fucker.

"And you want to be the one to do the killing."

I don't respond. Of course, I want to be the one to end Price's life.

"I thought you agreed Chrissie would contact her connections at the agency and let them know Price is alive, so they can do the hunting."

I grip the edge of the bar until my knuckles turn white. "I can't do it. I can't allow Chrissie to be in danger when I can find the man who's hunting her."

Max snorts. "Think a lot of yourself, don't you?" I glare at him. "You know as well as I do the agency has been hunting Price for years. There was no body. They knew damn well and good, he wasn't dead. But you're going to sweep in there and find him like that." He snaps his fingers.

I bare my teeth at him. "I don't have to follow the rules."

He chuckles. "Because they do?"

"Brother," Lenny says and waits for me to meet his eyes before continuing, "if you leave now, any progress you've made getting Chrissie to trust you is gone. She won't thank you for going after Price. She'll consider it as you abandoning her."

"What do you know about it? Where's your wife or husband?"

Pain flashes in his eyes before he locks it down.

"Fuck!" I shout before throwing my whisky glass across the room. It hits the wall and shatters. "I'm sorry, brother. I didn't mean…"

Lenny doesn't make me grovel. "I know."

Max clears his throat. "My soon-to-be wife is sleeping safely upstairs thanks to you, so I'll give you this. Lenny's right. You've been busting your ass to get Chrissie to give you a chance. Her faith in men has been destroyed by what Price did to her. You've got an opening right now to earn her trust and a place in her life. You leave? Whatever opening you've managed to create closes forever."

"He's not wrong," Sid chimes in. "With some women, you only get one chance. You waste your chance, it's over."

He's referring to his first wife. The woman who left him while he was deployed. He went AWOL to get back to her before she abandoned him, but he didn't make it in time. When he arrived home, she'd already packed up her shit and disappeared. He's spent years trying to fill the hole she left him with. We're all hoping Mary Ann is the one to fill the hole.

My chin drops to my chest. "I don't think I can do it. I feel like ants are crawling over my skin."

"A whiskey will help." Sid taps his chin. "Oh wait, you threw yours across the room."

Max plops another glass down on the bar in front of me. "And we'll help."

"Anytime you think you're going to explode, all you need to do is call." Lenny smirks. "I'll be glad to beat the crap out of you until you can't feel those ants anymore."

"As if you have a chance." If there's anyone who does have a chance, it's Lenny.

"Drink your whisky." Sid nods to the glass. "And then I'll beat your ass in pool. Mary Ann will shit a brick if I come home with scraps from a fight."

"She doesn't like to kiss your boo-boos?" Lenny mocks.

Sid waggles his eyebrows. "She'll kiss all my boo-boos and then some."

I smack him upside of the head. "You're talking about your wife, asshole."

His smile spreads from ear to ear. "And how are those ants feeling right now?"

Damn. The man is smarter than he appears. Considering the guy has blond hair and blue eyes and resembles a surfer, it's not saying much.

I down my whisky and let the warmth burn through me. I barely set the glass down before Max is filling it again. I shake my head. "I need to have a level head."

"This is your last one," he says before putting the bottle away.

I notice my brothers are drinking water. I know it's because they want to be clear-headed in case they need to have my back. Or unless they need to lock me down. As much as the idea of fighting all of them and leaving to hunt down Price appeals to me, I know they're right. Chrissie will never learn to trust me if I abandon her now.

And I need Chrissie to trust me because I'm never leaving her alone. I knew the minute I saw her, I wanted her. It only took one comment from her for me to want to fall to my knees at her feet. The woman is embedded in my heart and I'm not letting her go.

Chapter 21

What do a Russian spy and a teenager have in common? They both have erased history.

"Why was the guitar teacher arrested?" Barney asks as he escorts me to *You Cheat, We Eat* on Tuesday morning.

I hold up a hand to stop him from finishing the joke. We're outside the door to the office and I want to listen to ensure the place is empty before entering. Barney the jokester switches off and Barney the soldier replaces him.

I nod at him when I ascertain nothing is amiss, but before I can open the door, he pushes me out of the way. I glare at him.

"Wally will kill me if I let you enter an unknown situation first."

I frown. Wally. I am not happy with the man at the moment. He dropped me off at my house last night. Stood by while I called Lexi and filled her in on the situation. Then, he ensured Barney was in place before kissing my forehead and storming off. I haven't heard a word from him since.

"It's clear," Barney says when he exits Hailey's office. He frowns when he notices me standing in the reception area. "You were supposed to wait in the hallway."

I don't bother responding. If he hasn't figured out I'm not the type to wait in the hallway by now, he never will.

By the time Hailey and Phoebe arrive fifteen minutes later, Barney is settled into a chair with a newspaper and I'm finishing my first coffee of the day.

"Where's Ryker?" I ask the second they enter the reception area. It's a preemptive strike, but I don't have much hope it will be effective.

"He's going after a chase in Michigan. He should be back in a few days. Why is Barney here?" Phoebe asks.

Geez. My preemptive strike had zero effectiveness. "Sorry. Need to know."

Hailey nods. "Okay," she says and strolls into her office.

"Okay?" Phoebe shouts after her. "You can't seriously be satisfied with her answer."

When Hailey doesn't respond, Phoebe stomps her foot and marches into her office. I conceal my smile, but Barney notices and shakes his head at me.

The morning is quiet. Phoebe and Hailey hide out in their respective offices doing online searches while I enter expense report information into a spreadsheet. It's not exciting, but it's safe, which is what I need right now. Except I'm not safe here. I cut those thoughts off. Thinking about Flynn will not help anything.

The door opens and a woman enters. She surveys the reception area with wild eyes. When her gaze lands on mine, I smile. "Welcome to *You Cheat, We Eat.* How may I help you?"

Before I can ask, Barney abandons the chair in front of my desk and moves to lean against the wall opposite from me.

"You're a PI firm?"

I nod. "We are." At least she doesn't think we're a food delivery service. "Are you in need of a private investigator?"

"Oh god, yes." She collapses into a chair.

"What can we help you with?"

"My mind is being controlled."

I cock an eyebrow. Mind control exists, but somehow I don't think she's talking about the brainwashing I'm familiar with.

"Start at the beginning."

I hear Phoebe and Hailey creep toward the room, but I hold up a hand to stop their approach. I can handle this.

"I planned a trip to Peru to visit Machu Picchu this past summer."

When she doesn't say more, I prod her to open up, "Machu Picchu is very cool. Did you like it?"

"I never made it there. I got made redundant at work and lost my vacation days."

"I'm sorry."

"Thanks. Anyway, I got a vaccine for yellow fever thinking I was traveling to Peru. It's recommended." I nod. "And since then my mind has been controlled."

"Can you give me some examples?"

She sighs. "Oh, thank goodness, you believe me."

I don't believe her, but I like to have the facts before taking action. "Some examples," I prompt.

She glances over her shoulder at Barney, but he pretends to be immersed in his newspaper. She focusses on me again before whispering, "It started with small things like having cravings for food I don't like. You won't believe the amount of strawberry ice cream I've eaten and I don't even like strawberries."

"Hmm…" I pretend to be engrossed. "And then what happened?"

She leans closer. "I started wanting sex like all the time. And I identify as asexual."

My ears perk up. "Have you been forced to have sex against your will?" I hear Barney growl, and I throw him a glare.

She waves her hand. "No, no, no. I haven't actually had any sex lately, but I really, really want to, which is not normal."

"I'm not clear on how we can help you," I tell her.

"It gets worse. Suddenly, my mind is telling me to re-arrange all the furniture in my house. I've had the furniture arranged the same way for the past fifteen years. Obviously, someone is controlling my mind. This is not like me."

Oh boy. Someone's hopped on the crazy train. I roll my eyes and my gaze catches on Phoebe standing in the doorway eavesdropping. I can practically hear the snap of electricity as the lightbulb above my head goes off.

"Miss … I'm sorry I didn't get your name."

"Nancy. You can call me Nancy."

"Hi, Nancy. I'm Chrissie. Can I ask you a personal question?"

"Of course. As long as you believe me, you can ask me anything."

"You said you identify as asexual but have you had sex before?"

She grunts. "This is why I'm asexual. The last time I had sex was awful. Just awful."

"And this was when?"

Her brow wrinkles as she thinks about it. "Maybe six months ago."

"Sweetie, I think you're pregnant."

Her eyes widen and she shakes her head back and forth. "No, no, no. I can't be, can I?" She mumbles as she uses her fingers to count. "For crying out loud, I am." She stands. "I need to…" She hugs her bag to her chest but doesn't make any move to leave.

Barney steps forward and takes her elbow. "Let me escort you to the elevator."

As soon as the elevator pings its arrival on our floor, Hailey bursts out laughing. "How can she not know she's pregnant?"

Phoebe plops down on a seat in front of me. "Her poor child. She's going to forget all about him and leave him at school one day or maybe at a rest stop on the highway." She shivers.

"She'll be fine." Hailey sits next to her.

"I'm glad I didn't have to deal with her. The last time I had a crazy client, he raged about aliens stealing his sperm. I'll tell you about it sometime."

I look her in the eye and tell her, "Aliens are real."

Barney shouts, "I knew it!"

The door opens, and Valerie enters. Her gaze locks on Barney's before she asks him, "You knew what?"

Barney gulps and backs away. "Nothing."

Phoebe sighs. "I totally lost that bet. I thought Barney would jump Valerie before the end of Thanksgiving, but Christmas is coming up, and still nothing."

Valerie winks at her. "Don't worry. I'll wear him done eventually." She looks Barney up and down and licks her lips. All the color leaves the poor man's face.

Hailey studies the two. "I have New Year's Eve, but I think maybe I should switch to Valentine's Day. Everyone likes nookie on Valentine's Day. Plus, it's a wedding. Bridesmaids always nail the single groomsmen at weddings."

Barney appears as if he's about to faint. There's a story there, but he's not going to tell it in front of these blabbermouths.

"What's up, Valerie?" I ask instead of interrogating Barney.

"A little birdie told me Barney was here today. I thought I'd stop by and ask him if he wants to get some lunch together."

"It was me," Phoebe whisper-shouts. "I was the little birdie."

Hailey frowns. "Dude, you already lost the bet."

"Doesn't mean I can stop you from winning, though, does it?"

"Suzie's right. We created a monster." Hailey's eyes nearly pop out of her head when she realizes what she said. "No one tell Suzie I said she was right about something. I'll never hear the end of it."

Valerie struts over to Barney who's now plastered to the wall. She trails a finger down his chest. "What do you say, big boy? You want to get out of here and go grab something to eat?" She licks her lips. "I'm feeling awful peckish right now."

He gulps. "I c–c–can't."

Oh, for heaven's sake. What is wrong with the man? He's supposed to be my bodyguard? This is ridiculous. I stand.

"Sorry, Valerie. Barney has to stay here with me today."

Her hand drops and she backs up. "Sorry, Chrissie. I didn't realize you called dibs. I would never steal a man from a friend."

I motion to Barney. "He's all yours. We're not involved. He's working."

"And what's he working on?" Hailey asks.

I give her a full dose of the look. She cringes and drops her gaze. "Never mind."

Valerie bites her lip as she scans the room. She obviously doesn't understand what's going on, but I can't fill her in. It's bad enough I told Wally and his brothers. I'm not telling anyone else.

"Okay. I'll see everyone later then, I guess." She waves, gives Barney a wink, and leaves.

As soon as the door closes, Barney releases his breath. "She's terrifying."

I study Barney for a minute before saying, "I'll take New Year's Day."

"Traitor."

My body freezes, and my heart stops beating. I thought I could trust Wally's brothers to not only keep their mouths shut but to also understand what happened. Guess I was wrong.

"Shit." Barney runs a hand through his hair. "I'm sorry. You're not a traitor. It was a joke. An inappropriate joke."

My heart resumes beating, and I take a much needed breath. I force a smirk on my face. "I'm totally winning this bet."

Phoebe stands. "Not if I can help it," she mumbles as she returns to her office.

Hailey stands as well. She looks between us for a second. I know she's trying to figure out what just happened. Unlike Phoebe, she definitely noticed Barney's blunder. I smile at her, and she harrumphs before shutting herself in her office.

"I'm—"

I slash my finger across my throat to cut Barney off and then point to my ear. I can hear Hailey standing on the other side of her door. Barney places a hand on his heart and bows while mouthing *I'm an idiot.* I won't argue with his assessment.

My phone beeps, and I flip it over to read the text.

I'll see you at home.

I grunt. Wally ghosted me after my ex showed up and I opened my heart and revealed my deep, dark secrets and now he thinks he can just show up at my house. We'll see about that. I don't bother to respond before stowing my phone away.

Chapter 22

My wife thinks I should become a spy. She says I'm naturally good at moving in and out unnoticed.

WHEN BARNEY DROPS ME off at my house, Wally is already waiting for me in his truck. He opens his door as I walk up the drive, but I march right past him without saying a word. I am not talking to the jerk. How dare he show up here? Who does he think he is?

He grasps my arm to stop my movement, and I whirl around on him. "Don't you dare put your hands on me," I hiss.

He releases my arm and raises his hands in surrender. "Can we talk?"

"Now you want to talk? After ghosting me all night and all day? Guess what? Now, I don't want to talk to you."

He scrubs a hand down his face. "I fucked up."

"No shit. Are we done here?"

"Can I come inside and explain?" He swallows. "Please."

I open my mouth to tell him to take a hike straight to hell when I notice the curtain in the window at the old lady's house across the street flutter. Note to self: Next time I buy a house, do background checks on the neighbors first.

"Fine. You have five minutes," I say before resuming my march to my house.

The second the door opens, Gray meows and rushes to me. I pick her up for a cuddle as I disarm the alarm system. My kitty doesn't allow me to cuddle her for long before she jumps from my arms and stalks to the kitchen. She wants her dinner.

I get her settled on the floor with a can of wet food before grabbing a bottle of beer and returning to the living room where I find Wally studying the room as if he's memorizing every single thing.

"Tick tock."

He prowls toward me and doesn't stop until he's in my space. He reaches out but doesn't touch me when I snap my teeth at him.

"I'm sorry I didn't contact you earlier today. I spent the day passed out."

My brow wrinkles. Passed out? What the hell? Is he so unconcerned about me now he knows my story he can spend the entire day sleeping? Did I seriously consider trusting this guy? Goes to show you – I have horrible taste in men.

He frowns. "Whatever you're thinking, you're wrong."

I sip my beer to buy me time to wipe my face clear of emotions. "You have no clue what I'm thinking."

He grunts. "I'm not an idiot. I know you're pissed at me for disappearing on you after you told us about Price."

I flinch at *his* name. It's been a long time since I said his name out loud and now the name is out there and being thrown around all the dang time.

"I was passed out because my brothers got me drunk and had to carry me to my bed."

"Got you drunk? What the hell? I thought you were all geared up to keep me safe." I nearly swallow my tongue at those last words. Shit. Show him all your cards, why don't you, Chrissie?

He advances and I retreat until I hit a wall. He places his hands on the wall near my head but doesn't touch me. He leans close before saying, "I wanted to leave." I gasp. He was going to leave?

He places a finger over my mouth. "Let me get this out." I nod.

"I wanted to hunt Price." That makes more sense. "But my brothers pointed out I needed to stay here with you."

"Why?"

He moves his hand to tuck a strand of my hair behind my ear. "Because you need me here."

I glare at him. "I don't need you."

"Angel, you do. You were pissed when you thought I ghosted you all day." I tilt my head to the side to hide my reaction to the truth of his statement.

He cups my cheek and places gentle pressure on my jaw until I'm forced to meet his gaze. "I get it now. I didn't want to hear it when my brothers told me I needed to stay here and take care of you. I thought finding Price and killing him was taking care of you, but anyone can take care of Price. Only I can take care of you."

"Conceited much?"

"I'm not conceited, baby. What I am is the man in your house with you in my arms. And I don't need to be a genius to work out I'm the first man to get close since Price."

"Stop saying his name," I snarl.

Every time his name is uttered out loud, I remember what a fool I was to trust him – to love him. Except the feelings I had for him aren't anything close to how I feel about Wally after only a month of knowing him. Shit. Did I never love Price? Or did I convince myself I loved him because I was lonely? I shove those thoughts into a box in my mind and close and lock the lid. Now is not the time to have some big revelation about my past.

Wally nods. "Okay, Angel. I can give you that."

We stand there gazing into each other's eyes for several long seconds before I give in and speak. "What now?"

"Now, I take care of you," he whispers before his lips meet mine.

His hand fists my ponytail. I gasp when he tugs on my hair, and he uses my surprise to push his tongue past my lips. His taste hits me and I forget all the reasons I don't want a relationship with a man. My hands wander from his shoulders down to squeeze his ass. He groans before thrusting against me.

My reaction to feeling his hard length press against my body is instantaneous. My panties get wet. My breasts feel heavy. My nipples tingle and my legs get weak. My head is swimming.

I lose my mind and hitch my right leg over his hip where I can grind myself against him. Wally releases my hair and yanks his lips from mine. "Hop up."

No need to tell me twice. I wrap my legs around his waist and moan at how good it feels to have his cock hitting my center right where I need it to. I let my head fall back to the wall as I grind myself against him.

"Bedroom or couch?"

I can't respond. I'm too busy enjoying the friction my grinding is creating. Wally's fingers dig into my hips to stop my movement.

"Bedroom or couch? Choose or I'll choose for you."

"Bedroom," I gasp.

"Hold on tight," he commands, and I tighten my arms and legs around him.

He marches through the hallway to my bedroom while carrying me like I weigh close to nothing. I'm five-foot-ten and have curves, I do not weigh nothing. But Wally isn't even breathing hard when he switches on the light in my bedroom.

"No light," I insist.

"I want to see your body while I lick every inch of it."

I shiver. Guess the light's staying on after all.

I expect Wally to throw me on the bed and pounce on me, but he doesn't. He lays me down before falling to his knees in front of me. He removes my socks, massaging my feet as he does so. Then, he kisses my toes and stands.

At the confused look upon his face, I ask, "What's wrong?"

"I didn't think this through. I want to undress you but you're wearing those painted on jeans."

I giggle before getting to my feet. "This better?"

His eyes flare. In place of speaking, he smirks before tearing the button of my jeans open and lowering the zipper. His hand dives into my panties and his finger lands on my clit. When he rubs circles around it, I moan.

"More," I demand.

His hand disappears, and I open my eyes to glare at him. "I said more."

He smirks. "And you'll get more. You'll get everything you need."

"Promises. Promises."

"Damn straight." He shoves my jeans and panties down my legs before helping me to step out of them and throwing them across the room. His hands glide along my skin as he stands. I shiver as goosebumps trail in the wake of his hands.

He reaches the hem of my sweater and yanks it up and over my head. I barely have time to lift my arms before it too is thrown across the room. I'm now standing naked in front of him except for my bra. And it's not one of those lacy bras you read about in romance novels. Those are uncomfortable as hell. Especially if you have to start running for your life.

"You're gorgeous. Every single inch of you."

My hand automatically moves to the scar on the back of my neck, but Wally captures my hand to stop me.

"Every single inch," he repeats before his lips find mine. He pins my hands behind my back as he ravages my mouth with his tongue. I fight back and my tongue duels with his. I arch my back and rub my chest against his until my nipples form hard peaks.

"You're a vixen," he whispers against my mouth.

Actually, I'm not, but Wally brings it out in me. I'm not telling him that, though. He doesn't need any more ammunition than he already has.

He rips his mouth from mine. "Are you trying to make sure this is over before I can get my pants off?"

"I guess it's time to remove your pants then, Bossy," I challenge.

Now, he does throw me on the bed. I giggle as I bounce. The amusement dies as I watch Wally strip. No one would believe this man is nearly sixty. His body is a work of art. Defined muscle without an ounce of fat anywhere.

He pushes his jeans and boxers down and his cock pops out. Goodie. It's time for the main attraction. I reach behind me and unsnap my bra before throwing it across the room where it joins the rest of our discarded clothing.

Wally climbs on the bed but stops and swears. "Damn."

"What's wrong?" I cock my head and listen for an intruder, but I hear nothing.

"Condom," he grunts.

"Not necessary. It's not like you can get me pregnant. And I haven't had sex since…" I wave my hand. I'm not saying *his* name in the bedroom while naked with another man.

"I'm clean, but I'll get tested before I take you bare. It's another way for me to keep you safe."

I nearly melt at his words. Damnit. Can he stop being sweet already? I can't handle sweet.

He fiddles with his jeans until he finds his wallet and removes a condom. He dons the protection before joining me once again on the bed.

I widen my legs in invitation and he settles himself between them with his cock bumping my clit. I groan and arch my back. "Feels good."

"Angel, this is nothing," he says as he guides himself inside.

I reach behind me and grasp the headboard before wrapping my legs around his hips. When I arch my back to try and force him to hurry up, he freezes.

"I'm in charge in the bedroom."

I tilt my head down to meet his gaze and smirk. "Like hell you are." I use my legs to flip us over until I'm on top of him. I grasp his length and lower myself until he's fully seated inside me.

Wally moans and his eyes close. l rise up, but before I can slam down on him, his hands squeeze my hips to stop me.

"Slow. I want to enjoy our first time together."

I lean down to kiss his lips. "You will, Bossy. I promise."

He chases my lips, but I sit up and place my hands on his abs for leverage. I start lifting and lowering myself on him. I'm not going to last long. It never takes long for me to come this way. And with Wally's fingers digging into my hips leaving bruises, I'm going to come faster than I ever have before.

I feel my breasts bounce up and down, and I lift my hands to toy with my nipples. Wally growls. "That's my job."

I lean over him until my breasts are in his face. "Then, get to work, soldier."

While one hand kneads one breast, his mouth devours the other one. When his teeth nip at my nipple, I'm done. I quicken my pace as I pant.

"Almost there."

His fingers toy with my nipple and I ignite. I tighten around him as every nerve ending in my body explodes and my toes curl.

"Yes," I moan.

It's only when I collapse on him that I realize Wally came with me and he's gasping for breath as much as I am.

"Not bad for an old man," I pant out.

Wally growls and flips us until I'm underneath him. "I'll show you who's an old man."

Oh, goodie!

Chapter 23

What's a spy's favorite holiday? Halloween! It's all about the spooks.

I EXTEND MY ARMS above my head as I stretch my body upon waking the next morning. My body is deliciously sore in places it hasn't been sore in too freaking long. Wally shifts until he's on top of me.

"Good morning, Angel," he whispers before kissing my lips.

I wind my legs around him to discover he's wearing underwear. "When did you get dressed?"

He chuckles. "Wearing boxers is hardly dressed."

"Maybe not, but it's a barrier to the goods," I pout.

He kisses my nose. "Now, this is how I want to wake up every morning."

I freeze. "We're not in a relationship."

"You naked in bed with me says otherwise."

Crap. I'm weak. Why did I succumb to having sex with him? Succumb? Seriously, Chrissie. You practically attacked the man. True story. But he's sexy and hard to resist and wants to keep me safe and I think I trust him. Double crap.

I try a different tactic. "You're nearly sixty and have never been married. You can't seriously want a relationship right now."

He shrugs. "I've never wanted a relationship before this."

"And now you do?" I don't believe him.

"Hell yeah, I do. I've never met anyone who I know can understand what I do. Who won't bitch and complain when I can't tell her what I'm doing at work. But you do."

"Summing up, you want to be with me because I'm a former spook who understands what it's like to be in a relationship with a spook." Color me unimpressed.

He grasps my chin. "No, Angel. I want to be with you because you're gorgeous and smart and loyal as hell. You're also sexy as all get out and get my engines revving like no woman before."

"Engines revving? How old are you again?"

He grins but doesn't respond to my lame ass attempt to distract him. "You knowing what I do for a living and being able to handle it elevates you from casual relationship to my forever girl."

"Forever. Hold up. You went from relationship to forever awful fast."

"Baby, we had the children talk already."

"Which was really weird considering our ages."

"You're forty-nine, not ninety-nine. You have a lot of living left in you, and I plan to spend the rest of my days tied to you."

I gulp. "Tied to me? Like marriage?" My stomach rolls. This conversation is going places I'm not prepared to go to right now.

I don't know if I'll ever be prepared to go there. The last time marriage was in the picture was a disaster after all.

"You don't want to get married? We'll live in sin for the rest of our lives. But, just saying, I want you to have my last name."

I need to put the brakes on this conversation. We've hardly known each other a month and had sex for the first time last night. It is way too early to be having the marriage and children talk. I'll think about this later. Like when I don't have a nearly naked man in my bed. A man who proved his sexual prowess last night with spectacular results.

I arch my back and rub my breasts against Wally's chest. "Since we're both naked, or nearly naked, I have a few ideas of what we can do."

He groans and leans his forehead against mine. "As much as I'd like to hear about those ideas, you need to get to work."

I sigh. Hailey, Phoebe, and Ryker are all out of the office today, so it's up to me to be at *You Cheat, We Eat* to man the office. I worried I was going to hate being chained to a desk job, but it hasn't bothered me before. Until today.

"You're no fun," I pout to hide my disappointment.

He rolls off the bed taking me with him. "Let me show you how much fun I can be in the shower."

"Race you," I shout before running into the attached bathroom as fast as I can.

I check my watch as I finish brushing out my hair. After an extended shower with Wally, I'm going to be late. I'm finding it hard to care. It was totally worth it.

I finish putting my hair in a ponytail and head toward the kitchen. I need food before I leave for the office. I screech to a halt when I notice my living room. Or at least this used to be my living room.

"What the hell?" I shout as I hear Wally approach behind me.

He wraps his arms around my middle from behind me and rests his chin on my shoulder. "Do you like it?"

"How did you do this? When did you do this?"

Someone barfed Christmas all over my living room. There's a tree in the corner, stockings are hung over the mantel, garland and lights decorate the fireplace, a wreath is on my door, there are red pillows on my couch as well as a blanket with a snowman on it, and there's a poinsettia on my coffee table.

"Phoebe bought the decorations for me, and I put them up last night."

"Last night? When did you have time last night?" I barely got any sleep considering how many sexy times we had.

He waggles his eyebrows at me. "I think you've figured out by now I have a lot of stamina."

"Stamina and not needing sleep are two different things," I point out.

He grasps my hand to lead me into the room. "What do you think?"

"It's nice." I guess. "But why?"

He drops down on the sofa taking me with him. He situates me on his lap before hugging me close. "Because I want to give you everything. I know it was hard for you to tell me about your parents and how they died at Christmas."

I open my mouth to tell him it wasn't hard, but I stop when I realize I'd be lying. It *was* difficult to tell him about my family. I've never told anyone except Lexi before about how my parents died and she found out by accident because she got me drunk on moonshine when I visited her family in West Virginia one holiday season. I never even considered telling Flynn what happened.

I pause at that thought. If ever there was a big red sign pointing out how I didn't love Flynn, this is it. But I did tell Wally. I hadn't even known the man long before I entrusted him with my secret. Shit. The man is embedding himself under my skin and I didn't even realize it.

"Did you—"

He shakes his head. "Of course, I didn't tell anyone about your parents. It's your story to tell."

"Thank you." I study all the changes in my living room. "For everything, although the Christmas tree is sad. It's like a Charlie Brown Christmas tree."

He laughs. "I thought we could decorate it together. It's what families do."

Oh boy. He went from relationship to family in warp speed.

"You need to slow down. My head is spinning, and I can't keep up."

Wally studies my face for a moment before nodding. "Okay. I'll stop pushing you about forever as long as we're dealing with Price."

I smile. "Deal."

"I wasn't finished."

I roll my eyes. Of course, he wasn't.

"In the meantime, we're in a relationship."

"Friends with benefits?" I can hope, can't I?

"Call it what you want, but you won't be calling any other man as long as I'm in your bed."

"Bossy, don't make me mad." I told him last night I haven't been with another man since Price.

"And I won't be with another woman as long as we're together."

"Not if you like your balls right where they are, you won't."

He leans close to whisper in my ear. "I'm not the only one who likes my balls where they are."

I shove him away and stand. "I need to get to work."

"Lenny's on you today."

I want to protest. I know I can handle myself in all kinds of dangerous situations, but I also know Price is sneaky. He blew up a building, killing nearly fifty people, to allow him to disappear. He doesn't care about collateral damage. A man with nothing to lose is a dangerous man.

"Where are you off to?"

"Need to know, Angel," he says and then braces.

"Gotcha," I say, and his shoulders deflate. "As long as it doesn't involve me, I will never ask you to divulge information you're not free to divulge."

I'm not saying this because we're in a relationship. I'm saying this because this is who I am. Even before I went to work for the agency, I wasn't one to pry. I don't like it when people pry into my personal business. I'd be a hypocrite if I pried into theirs.

"Thanks, Angel."

My stomach rumbles. "I'm starving and I can smell bacon. Feed me before I have to leave for work."

Chapter 24

Beer. Because you don't win friends with salad.

AFTER FINISHING UP AT *You Cheat, We Eat,* Lenny drives me to Suzie's beer shack. She called everyone and declared a national beer emergency. After I insisted there is no such thing as a national beer emergency, she explained how she has a huge order to fill but ruined her first batch of Christmas Ale. Something about cleanliness. I honestly didn't bother trying to understand. Beer is for drinking. I don't care how it's made as long as it's cold.

I pause in front of the building. "Holy cow. This isn't a shack."

The building is a large warehouse with a neon sign for Shorty's Brewing Sensation with her logo underneath it.

"Once Grayson pulled Suzie's head out of her ass, things snowballed from there."

I wasn't around when Grayson and Suzie fell in love, so I don't know the whole story. I do know Grayson also had his head up in the ass about some event from when he was deployed. Like I said, I don't pry. If people want to tell me their stories, I'll listen. But I don't ask questions.

A car door slams, and I turn to watch as Valerie hurries our way. "Is Barney here?" she asks but doesn't wait for a response before continuing into the building.

"She didn't give you a second glance."

As far as I know, Lenny is single. He and Barney are the only single men left of the brothers. And Wally, I remind myself. Although, after this morning's 'we're serious' discussion, I'm finding *that* particular lie difficult to swallow.

Lenny chuckles. "Let Barney have her. She terrifies me."

I giggle. "Barney is pretty terrified of her himself."

Wally palms my neck before kissing my hair. "Hey, Angel. You don't seem surprised to find me here."

"A blind man could hear your approach, Bossy."

Truth is, I didn't exactly hear him, but when I saw Lenny glance over my shoulder and my body warmed, I knew it had to be Wally. How my body is attuned to him in such a short time is not a question I want to think about right now, though.

"What are we here for anyway?" I ask as we enter the building. "I don't know anything about brewing beer."

Wally opens his mouth to answer but Suzie shrieks and rushes toward us. Grayson trails behind her, his arms out to catch her in case she falls as if she's a baby taking her first steps. Watching the nearly six-foot-tall former soldier with his linebacker build chase after munchkin Suzie would be hilarious if it weren't for the expression of sheer panic on his face.

"Wally and Chrissie had sex! Who had today?"

"Yesterday," Wally corrects her, and I elbow his stomach hard enough he grunts at the force.

Faith's hand shoots into the air. "I did."

I cock an eyebrow at her and her cheeks darken. "Sorry, but this betting with the brothers is kind of addictive."

I decide to give her a break. "I've got New Year's Day for Valerie and Barney."

"I've got Christmas for them."

I hear Barney gulp behind me. The man is such a scaredy-cat. I shake Faith's hand. "May the best woman win."

Wally squeezes my neck. "I think you mean person."

I snort. "Um, no. I mean woman. If I don't win, Faith will. You wait and see."

"Can we stop talking about my love life now?" Barney squeaks.

"Alrighty! Let's talk about how Chrissie slayed Wally's dragon last night." Suzie wiggles her fingers. "I want all the deets."

Grayson groans. "We've talked about this. No details about other people having sex."

Suzie makes a talking motion with her hand. "Talk. Talk. Talk. I never agreed."

Phoebe and Hailey enter with Aiden and Ryker. "What are we talking about?" Phoebe asks.

Suzie smirks. "Wally and Chrissie having sex."

Phoebe feigns gagging. "No. I don't want to hear about Wally having sex. He's like a father to me."

Wally frowns. "Which is why you asked Pops to escort you down the aisle instead of me?"

Max chuckles. "Brother. She said you're like a father to her. I am a father to her."

As far as I understand it, Phoebe's family is a den of complete and total asshole vipers. When she married Ryker, her parents weren't even invited. The brothers went crazy courting Phoebe to convince her to pick one of them to escort her down the aisle. Max won out, and it's not hard to figure out why. He has a daughter, and he treats Phoebe like one.

Faith wraps an arm around Max. "Which is why I can't have girl talk with Phoebe about Max in the bedroom."

Phoebe pales. "Please. Stop. I'm begging you."

Valerie lifts her hand. "I vote no to stopping. I have no problems imagining what Max the man is like in bed. And I do more than imagine if you get my drift." She licks her lips and winks at Barney.

Barney gulps before taking a step back. Valerie advances on him. He spins around and rushes off with Valerie chasing him. Idiot. Doesn't he realize she gets off on the chase?

I clap my hands. "As much as I enjoy witnessing Phoebe squirm and Barney going all scaredy-cat, I believe we're here for a reason. Suzie?"

"I made a bit of a mistake with my batch of Christmas Ale," Suzie declares with a wrinkle of her nose. "FYI – if you're pregnant, do not rely on your nose when mixing a batch of beer. It's not to be trusted."

She stares at Phoebe who shrugs and states, "I don't even drink beer."

"Anyway," Grayson finishes up the story. "We're behind on our deliveries and, with the holidays, we've had more orders than usual. With just me and klutzy girl, we'll never finish on time."

"What do you need us to do?" Wally asks. My belly warms at the idea of him rushing to help his friends. I glare at my belly. Stop it, I order.

Suzie starts bossing everyone around. We don hairnets and lab coats and get to work. Five minutes into labeling, I'm regretting wearing a sweater. My brow is damp, and my hands are clammy. Clammy hands and sticking labels on beer bottles do on go together.

"I'll be back," I tell Hailey before going in search of a restroom.

Before I can close the door behind me, a body shoves its way inside. I don't scream because my body knows it's Wally. The hussy is highly attuned to his presence.

He locks the door behind him before stalking toward me. I end up plastered against the wall. He wastes no time before his lips find mine. My hands lift and I scratch his scalp as he plunders my mouth. He grasps my waist and lifts me up forcing me to wrap my legs around his waist.

Someone pounds on the door. "No sexy times in the restroom until the bottling and labeling is done," Suzie shouts.

"And afterwards?" I can't resist asking.

"There are condoms under the sink."

I bury my face in Wally's shoulder as I laugh at her announcement. "Is she serious?"

"It's Suzie. I wouldn't put it past her."

I lean back to smile up at Wally.

"There she is, my Angel."

"I think we know by now I'm no angel, Bossy."

He winks. "You're my angel."

"Whatever." I try to get down, but he doesn't let me.

"Give me a minute."

"Dude, if you're waiting for the sausage in your pants to deflate, this stance isn't going to help." I rub myself against him and his cock jerks proving my point.

"Sausage?" He nips my neck. I tilt my head to give him better access. He licks the area before kissing and biting his way to my ear. "Missed you," he whispers.

"You saw me this morning," I protest despite missing him all day as well. How can I be addicted to this man in such a short time? It's terrifying.

"And I didn't get a chance to get my fill of you then. I'm never going to get my fill of you."

I don't shiver at his words. It's the sweat on my brow cooling down now I'm not working in a hot warehouse is all.

"We should get out there and help. I don't shirk my duties."

He lets me down and steps back. I immediately miss his warmth and regret having to help Suzie out. We could be at home snuggling on the sofa right now or doing naughty things to each other in bed. I'm leaning toward naughty things. We'll snuggle on the sofa together in a year or two after we slow down.

Year or two? This isn't a relationship, Chrissie. Yeah, yeah, and I'm not lying to myself.

Wally grasps my hand and opens the door. Hailey nearly falls inside the room. I shake my head at her. "Have you learned nothing from Suzie on how to eavesdrop? Didn't you hear us coming?"

She scans my body before turning around and shouting, "They didn't have sex! Who had no sex?"

"Your friends are crazy," I tell Wally.

"Not, my friends. Our friends."

I want to disagree with him. These people can't possibly be my friends. I hardly know them. But when Hailey looks over at me and winks, I know he's right. This group of oddballs adopted me into their gang, making me realize how long it's been since I had anyone who had my back.

I didn't realize how much I needed their friendships until they offered them without wanting anything in return. I glance at Wally. And maybe I need him, too.

Chapter 25

Who was the skeptical man who dressed up as a woman to spy on the Wright Brothers initial flight test? Mrs. Doubtflyer.

WALLY

"I need to go after Price," I declare to my brothers. I called them to meet at McGraw's Pub before it opens for lunch. If I'm in the wind, I need them to be on board with the plan, because I will not leave Chrissie unprotected.

Lenny sighs. "Didn't we have this conversation already?"

"I can't live like this. I can't live with Chrissie in danger." I scrub a hand down my face as I imagine Chrissie being kidnapped by Price. He'd torture her and maybe— I shake my head to stop my thoughts from going down that particular road.

"Brother," Max pauses until I meet his gaze. "We've got Chrissie covered. Someone is on her 24/7."

"But—"

The door bangs open, and I whirl around with my gun raised to find Chrissie standing in the doorway glaring at me.

"A secret meeting to discuss my stalker problem? I guess my invite got lost in the mail."

I holster my weapon. "How did you find out?"

She cocks her brow. "Are you serious? I'm kind of insulted by the lack of effort you made to hide this meeting. Do you have no faith in my skills, or did you subconsciously want me to find out?"

I grimace. "Subconsciously want you to find out."

Chrissie snorts. "Correct answer, Mr. Bossy."

I march to her and palm her neck to bring her close. "I told you I'm going to rock this relationship thing."

Her eyebrow scrunches. "Relationship thing? Then, this isn't a real relationship?"

I growl. "This is real. Don't you dare doubt it."

To prove it, I slam my lips on hers. She doesn't hesitate to open to me, and I dive right into her mouth. I've never been much into kissing. I'd rather go straight to getting naked, but kissing Chrissie is different. I could spend all night exploring her mouth with our clothes on. If I needed any proof my feelings for this woman are real, then those thoughts would have done it.

Max clears his throat. "Are we done here?"

"Yes," Chrissie shouts while I shout, "No!"

I glare at her. "We need to catch Price."

"Okay. I'm in. What's your plan?"

I blink. "What?"

"Plan. Do you need me to spell it out for you? P-L-A-N. Aka a proposal for how to accomplish your objective. The objective here being the capture of Flynn fucking Price."

"You are not going to be involved in any plan," I snap at her.

She pushes away from me and addresses my brothers. "What have you got thus far?"

Barney chuckles. "Thus far, we have Wally acting like a caveman."

"Why don't we give the powers that be a chance to find Price before we take over?" Max suggests. "It's only been three days."

Chrissie rolls her eyes. "If you think it's only been three days since they've been hunting Price, then you're wrong."

Max smirks. Chrissie is saying the exact same thing he said mere days ago. Damn. I was an idiot to not include her in this meeting from the start. She knows Price better than any of us, plus she's a highly trained operative. I squeeze her shoulder in support.

"Do you have any ideas?" I ask her.

She glances over her shoulder at me and her eyes warm. Yeah, trusting in her is the right thing to do.

"I hate to say it, but there's no way we can sniff out where Price is hiding."

"Explain," I order.

"If Price doesn't want to be found, he won't be." I open my mouth to contradict her, but she holds up a hand to stop me. "I know you're probably an expert at finding people who don't want to be found, but we don't have the proper resources."

I cross my arms over my chest. "I have resources."

"And you can't use them for this."

Crap. She's right. I don't have orders to find Price meaning I can't use all my usual resources. And, if I try to call in favors, the top will know what I'm up to and order me off the chase. Deputy Director Cruz already made it crystal clear I wasn't to act on my knowledge of Price being alive.

"But you have an idea," Lenny says when the silence drags on.

Chrissie smiles. "I do." The smile drops from her face when she looks at me. "But you're not going to like it."

There's only one thing I wouldn't like, and she knows it. "Hell no. You're not putting yourself in danger."

"I wouldn't be in danger. You guys have my back, don't you?"

Sid raises his hands and steps away. "No way. You're not putting us in the middle between you and Wally."

Chrissie huffs. "I'm not trying to put anyone in a tough spot. I'm saying using me as bait isn't dangerous because you would be keeping an eye on me." She frowns. "Or would you not have my back?"

Max snorts. "You're good."

She beams. "I was taught by the best."

I need to shut this shit off. "It's not happening."

Chrissie puts her hands on her hips and glares at me. "Okay. What is your bright idea, Mr. Bossy?"

"Simple. Find Flynn Price and make him regret the day he was born."

"And how do you plan to find Flynn when you have no resources? Do you know how long it took me to find him when he went rogue?"

My body vibrates in anger. I can't believe she ruined her career for this asshole. When I find him, I'm going to make it abundantly clear how a man does not hurt his woman by allowing her to ruin her life for him. I will never allow Chrissie to hurt herself again. She's mine to take care of now. I should probably be freaked out by those words, but I'm not. I've known since the minute I met her, she's mine.

Chrissie places her hands on my cheeks and leans in close to whisper to me, "There's no need to be jealous. Trust me, I don't care about Flynn anymore. That bridge burned to the ground when he blew himself up."

I place my forehead against hers and take comfort in her touch for a moment before reaching up to caress the scar Price left her with. "I'm not jealous." She raises an eyebrow in disbelief. "I'm not. I'm pissed at Price, not jealous of him."

"Okay. I believe you. Now, will you believe me when I tell you the one way to catch him is to use me as bait?"

"I do believe you, but I don't want you in harm's way. I never want you in harm's way again."

"Then, you picked the wrong girl." She winks before stepping away from me, forcing me to drop my hand.

"What's your plan, Chrissie?" Max asks.

I scan the room and notice all my brothers are looking to Chrissie as if they trust she knows what she's talking about and can take care of herself. My heart clutches and then the fear I didn't realize I was holding onto about my brothers accepting Chrissie disappears. I know I choose well, but knowing my brothers agree means the world to me.

"Nothing elaborate. I'll make myself vulnerable a few times and see if Flynn takes the bait."

Her phone beeps and she removes it from her pocket. "Shit. It's Hailey. She's wondering where I am. I better go. She's worried."

We've kept Hailey and her friends in the dark about what's going on with Chrissie, but Hailey is no dummy. She knows there's an issue with Chrissie.

"Where did you tell her you were going?" I ask.

"I didn't. I snuck out when Phoebe started throwing up all over the place and Ryker rushed to help her."

I glare at Sid. He was supposed to be protecting Chrissie today.

"I didn't leave her unguarded. Ryker promised he'd keep her safe in my absence."

"Ryker's wife is pregnant. His priority is going to Phoebe. It's always going to be Phoebe." I can't be mad at Ryker. Not when my priority will always be Chrissie.

"Can you guys continue this pissing contest later? I need to get back to the office before Hailey comes storming over here."

"Does she know you're here?" I ask.

"As if it's hard to figure out where you guys have your super-secret meetings." I can hear the laughter in Chrissie's voice. I want to hear her laugh every single day for the rest of my life. But what if Price gets his hands on her? She outed him as a traitor. He'll want revenge and he won't be nice about it.

Chrissie points at me. "Stop! Whatever scary thoughts are running through your brain right now, put the brakes on. Nothing is going to happen to me."

"Not if I have anything to say about it," I grumble.

She smiles up at me. "Lucky for you, you do have something to say about it."

Sid groans. "Come on, Chrissie. Let's get you back to the office. I don't need to witness you and my brother make out again."

Barney feigns puking. "I agree. Watching our little sister make out with our brother is gross."

Lenny sighs. "How old are you two again?"

I ignore them and give Chrissie a quick, hard kiss before letting her go. "Be safe."

"I always am." She winks before leading Sid out of the building.

I have to lock down my body to stop myself from following them. I know Sid will die to keep her safe, but it doesn't stop the fear from coursing through my veins.

"Wait a few minutes," Max orders when I take my first step. I don't bother asking him what he's talking about. I won't insult him. "Let them drive out of the parking lot before you follow."

I know Chrissie said there isn't a chance of me finding Price, but I've still got to try. If he's trailing them now, I will find him.

Chapter 26

As I sat there scratching my ass, and spying on my neighbor washing her beaver, one thing crossed my mind. We have really weird pets in my neighborhood.

"I don't like this," Wally says into my ear.

I don't roll my eyes since I don't want to give off the vibe of some crazy lady having a conversation with herself. Instead, I cover my mouth with my arm and whisper back, "Too bad."

I drop my arm and scan the area for any sign of Flynn. It's not easy. The Milwaukee Holiday Lights Festival is in full swing with more than 500,000 sparkly lights displayed throughout the downtown area. Wally and the gang are scattered around the streets following me.

We're communicating via earpieces, and I even allowed Wally to put a tracking device on me in case the unexpected happens and Flynn manages to capture me. I was not surprised to discover Wally had all the necessary equipment for this operation.

I keep my pace slow and steady as I pretend to be fascinated with the various animated sculptures, interactive displays, and twinkling street décor. I usually don't participate in these Christmas type events. Not since my parents died at least.

Before then? Christmas was my favorite holiday. I love everything winter. Snow, skiing, sledding, hot chocolate, you name it I love it. Or I used to love it. Although, as I stroll down the streets, my boots crunching on the fresh snow, my breath visible in the air from the cold, I can feel a bit of the magic of the season coming back to me.

I shake my head. I need to stay alert right now. Not have some revelation about myself. I glance into a store window to check the reflection for any strange movements and spot a blond head behind me. My heart speeds up. Flynn is blond.

I pretend to be fascinated with an item in the window as I observe the man in the reflection come closer. His head swivels toward me and I hold my breath as I wait to catch a glimpse of his face.

My breath rushes out of me when I notice the man is young. He's probably not yet thirty. Flynn is in his fifties and the years haven't exactly been kind to him. Not like Wally who could easily be mistaken for a man in his forties rather than his actual age of fifty-nine.

Stop it, Chrissie! No comparing Wally and Flynn. There is no comparison. Wally is loyal and kind and wants to give me everything my heart desires. Flynn is a traitor who was always gruff with me. Even when he told me he loved me, he was gruff.

I scan the area and my gaze catches on Wally standing across the street. He cocks an eyebrow at me, and I shake my head. He nods before melting into the crowd once more. He easily blends into the crowd despite being a head taller than most of the people.

I spend another hour meandering around downtown before calling it quits. "I'm going to the gym," I say into my earpiece as I open my car door.

"We didn't agree to this," Wally responds.

"Yeah, well, we're idiots. Flynn knows I'm not the type of woman to spend an hour strolling around a Christmas light display."

I never told my ex I hated Christmas, but he's no fool. He knows I never celebrated the holiday. He just doesn't know why, because he never asked. And if him not asking wasn't a sign flashing red flag, I don't know what was.

"We need to stick to my routine if we want him to come after me."

Which is the exact point I argued when the brothers converged on *You Cheat, We Eat* the second Hailey left this afternoon. Wally was having none of it. He doesn't want me to be in a gym with too many entry and exit points for them to cover.

After an hour of arguing, I gave in to the 'stroll through the Christmas lights display'-plan. Aka the 'stupid plan I knew would never work'. But when Wally refused to believe me, I knew I had to show him I was right.

"I'm heading to the gym," I tell him now. "Where I should have been all along," I can't help myself from adding.

"You're asking for a spanking," Wally grumbles into my ear.

"Now, we're talking," Sid shouts, and I cringe at the loud ringing his shout causes in my earpiece.

"I want details," Barney chimes in. "How often does he spank you? Does he only spank you when you're bad? Or is it an ongoing thing?"

"As if Chrissie lets Wally spank him," Lenny says and earns my devotion.

Damn right, I don't let Wally spank me. I'm not against a bit of rough play in the bedroom but spanking crosses a line for me. I don't care what anyone says, a man spanking me makes me feel like I'm powerless. And I refuse to ever be powerless.

"Can we stop talking about my love life and convince Chrissie to go home instead of to the gym?"

I burst into laughter at Wally's request. As if he can convince me to do anything. I can let him try, though.

"Why shouldn't I go to the gym? No one in the gym is going to let some strange man cart me off like it's nothing."

I don't belong to one of those fancy gyms with saunas and juice bars and whatever else people who like to pretend to work out but don't bother to break a sweat like. I'm a member of a fight gym where I lift weights and practice my boxing.

"We can't cover you in the women's locker rooms or re-strooms."

Wally sounds like a broken record. He only mentioned this concern about a thousand times earlier today. I wish I was exaggerating, but I'm not.

"And like I told you earlier, I can take care of my damn self."

"Unless Price surprises you or drugs you."

Flynn never was one to drug a suspect. He likes his suspects conscious and painfully aware of what's happening when he interrogates them. He gets off on his power over them.

"Too late. I'm here." I pull into the parking lot of the gym, grab my bag, and march to the front door before Wally can stop me.

"We're in place," Lenny whispers into my ear. I knew I could trust them. I nod before opening the door.

Despite my proud words to Wally, I'm not stupid. I wait until the only other woman in the place heads to the changing rooms before joining her. I know I'm at my most vulnerable in the changing room since the fight gym is nearly exclusively male.

I change as fast as I can, which is pretty fast considering my training and exit the changing room into the hallway. I glance to the left where the exit is and nod when I spot Barney standing guard there.

I skip the weights and head to the treadmill. I need to expend some of this anxiety from my body before I get jittery and make a mistake. I'm on my fourth mile when I spot him. Flynn leans against the mirror in the weight area with his arms crossed over his chest. He's not here to capture me – at least not yet. He's here to let me know he's watching me. It's a scare tactic and I'm not impressed.

"Target is on the premises," I mutter into my earpiece. "Weight area."

I slow my pace and keep my eyes trained on Flynn. What did I ever see in the guy? He's handsome enough with his blond hair and blue eyes. Add on his square jaw and stocky build and he didn't have to work hard to seduce me. I should have looked closer. His blue eyes are a gorgeous bright color, but they're also dead. And his smirk isn't sexy. It's creepy.

Wally appears and makes his way toward Flynn. Wally is stealth defined, but Flynn has a radar for when someone's stalking him. It's how he's survived this long. He smirks and waves at me through the mirror before turning and ambling away as if he's got all day. Wally gives chase.

I slam the emergency stop button on the treadmill and jump off it before sprinting after them. I chase them down the back hallway and out the emergency exit. The alarm doesn't go off telling me this isn't the first time Flynn has been in this gym.

When I exit the building into the cold Wisconsin December, I discover Wally standing in the middle of the parking lot with his weapon raised.

"I lost him. I fucking lost him." He marches to me. "Get your ass inside. You're sweating and it's freezing out here."

He grabs my upper arm and starts dragging me to the door. I wrench my arm free.

"I know you're mad you lost Flynn, but don't you dare try to move me against my will again."

Wally freezes, his eyes full of confusion before he lifts his head to the sky and swears as loud as he can. When he's wrestled himself back into control, he approaches me with his hands raised.

"I'm sorry, Angel. I didn't mean to force you. I needed to protect you, but I didn't go about it the right way."

I cross my arms over my chest for warmth, because it is freezing out here. "I accept your apology, but hear this – if it happens again, I will kick your ass."

"I have ten bucks on Chrissie," Lenny says.

Sid shrugs out of his coat and wraps it around my shoulders. Wrong thing to do. Wally growls before whipping his sweater off. He yanks Sid's coat away and throws it at him before lifting my arms to dress me in his sweater. I let him, because I know he's on edge. Besides, the sweater smells like Wally – fresh pine with a hint of musk.

"At least, we've confirmed Flynn Price is the man who's been stalking Chrissie," Max adds as he joins our huddle in the parking lot.

"I can't believe the fucker got away."

Wally's growling like a grizzly bear. I pet his chest and his growls slow before stopping completely. He wraps me in his arms.

"I will get him," he vows. "I won't let my woman be in danger."

"I know," I tell him.

And I do. This man was born to be a protector. And I probably should admit – at least to myself – that I'm his to protect. I gulp. Even admitting it to myself is terrifying.

Chapter 27

I caught a gorilla spying on me. I told him, "There is no need to pry mate".

I consult the clock on the kitchen wall when Wally stands to check the windows once again and sigh. It's been less than fifteen minutes since his previous check. I thought he would calm down once we were in my house with the door locked and the alarm engaged. I thought wrong.

"Maybe I should stay in a safe house until you find Flynn," I suggest.

"Good idea." He pulls out his phone. "I'll make the arrangements."

I stand and yank the phone out of his hand. "I was being sarcastic. Christina Lindberg doesn't hide."

"I know. I know you're a strong woman, but this is torture knowing you're in danger."

I squeeze his hands. "I'm not in danger. All the brothers plus Aiden, Ryker, and Grayson are watching out for me."

After we missed capturing Flynn at the gym, Wally insisted on adding more manpower to the group of people guarding me. I didn't argue, since I knew it would be a waste of breath. The husbands of my friends didn't hesitate to agree to help out. They don't know what exactly is going on, and Ryker and Grayson didn't bother asking questions. Aiden, however, tried pulling his police detective card and asked several questions until Wally pulled out the top-secret card, which trumps police detective card every single time.

I hope Aiden can keep his mouth shut with his wife. Otherwise, Hailey is going to be on my ass trying to figure out what's going on. And once Hailey is involved, Suzie will get involved and Phoebe won't be far behind them. I could do without the third degree.

"You saw Flynn today. He was practically mocking us."

"Such an asshole."

"Do you think he's working alone?"

"Who would work with him? Any American who cooperated with him would be labeled a traitor and never get another day's work again, and I don't think the Russians would come on American soil to help him in his little revenge plan."

"I hope you're right."

I hope so, too. In the dark world I used to inhabit, it was impossible to know who to trust and where allegiances lay. I sure as hell didn't figure Flynn for a traitor. He never had one good thing to say about the Russians. Of course, I realize now it was a ruse. I should have paid closer attention, but I was desperate for a connection.

"Come on." I grasp Wally's hand and lead him to the couch. "We're as safe as we can be right now. Two men will be outside all night long."

He jumps to his feet and starts pacing again. I sigh. I thought I had him calmed down for a minute there.

"It's not enough. I need an army to protect the woman I love."

Whoa. Wait. Did he say he loves me? "You love me?" It was a slip of the tongue. It has to be. He can't possibly love me.

He scoffs. "Of course, I love you."

"No. You've known me for like a minute. You can't be in love."

"Angel, I knew you were the one the second you laughed in my face after meeting me."

It's true. I did laugh in his face the first time I met him. I walked into McGraw's Pub to meet Hailey and the rest of the girls, he approached and gave me the lamest pick-up line of all time. *Hey, beautiful. I haven't seen you around here before.* I couldn't have stopped myself from laughing if I'd tried. And I didn't try.

"And then you bumped Barney's fist after he made some lame joke, and I felt a burn in my stomach. It took me a while to realize I was jealous of my own brother. I want all your smiles directed at me for the rest of my life, not at one of my brothers."

"Me smiling at Barney is what made you turn into a raging lunatic? You were jealous?"

I barely got a chance to sit down with Hailey and Suzie before Wally started demanding my information. I gave him my name and offered him my social security number, knowing full well he wouldn't get anywhere with a background check.

"Angel, until my ring is on your finger and you're carrying my last name, I'm going to have jealousy issues."

I spring to my feet and back away from him with my hands held out in front of me. "Stop right there! Marriage? You confessed to loving me less than five seconds ago and now you're talking marriage? When was your last psych eval?"

He chuckles as he advances on me. "Five months ago. Do you want to see the results?"

"Did you see the results? Maybe the psychologist mixed your name up with someone else? Someone who's sane." I keep retreating as I throw my questions at him.

I hit the kitchen counter and Wally doesn't hesitate to crowd me with his hands braced on each side of me near my hips. I can feel my chest rise and fall as I gasp for air. This is too much. It's too soon. I don't know if I'll ever be ready to make myself vulnerable to a man again. And this man standing in front of me staring into my eyes will demand everything I have to give. I know it.

He cups my chin. "Breathe, baby. You're going to hyperventilate if you don't calm down."

"You calm down," I say back like I'm an idiot.

Wally smirks.

"Oh, shut it."

His smirk grows into a smile. It stretches from ear to ear and lights up his eyes.

"What are you happy about?" Good grace. I've become a belligerent teenager. Is this what they mean with a mid-life crisis?

"I'm happy because the woman I love is standing right in front of me."

"You have to stop saying you love me." Every time the words leave his lips, I feel like I'm going to burst out of my skin.

"Angel, I'll give you everything you want in this world. The shirt off my back, every cent I have in the bank, all my time and attention, but I won't give you that. I won't lie to you."

"It's not lying. It's keeping your mouth shut. There's a difference." See what I mean? Belligerent teenager.

"I promise I'm not him."

"Of course, you aren't," I sneer at him. "I'm not an idiot. I know you're not a traitor. I trust you."

His eyes close and his forehead falls against mine. "Thank you, Angel."

Damnit. What is wrong with me? I shouldn't have told him I trust him. I mean, it's true. But I should have kept my mouth shut. Telling him I trust him is only going to encourage him more. And Wally doesn't need any encouragement as it is.

"I didn't mean—"

He places a finger over my mouth to stop me. "No, you're not taking back your words. I won't let you. And, Angel, I trust you, too."

"I know you do."

He wouldn't have ever let me walk alone down East Wisconsin Avenue tonight if he didn't. And he definitely would have stopped me from entering the gym otherwise.

"Then, trust me to know how I feel. I'm fifty-nine years old. I've waited a long time to find you. I'd nearly given up on finding you. Hear this, I will not waste one more minute now that you know how I feel."

His words pierce through my heart and my body warms as my nerves tingle. He's saying everything I ever wanted a man to say to me. Except for the fifty-nine years old thing. I never thought I'd need nearly half a century to find love.

Wait. I haven't found love. I haven't known Wally long enough to know if I love him. Except I trust him. I trust him to keep me safe. Something I never trusted Flynn to do, despite our years together and our declarations of love.

My head spins with all the revelations being made today. Those Wally made out loud. And those I'm making to myself in my head.

"We need to slow down."

Wally winks. "I can go slow," he says before dipping his head. His lips bypass mine and land on my neck. He nibbles and bites his way from my neck to my ear. And I, hussy that I apparently am, tilt my head to give him better access.

He bites my earlobe and I moan. "Is this slow enough for you?"

He rolls his hips, and his hard length pushes against my belly. "Not slow," I pant as he continues to rock into me.

"Our clothes are on. Thus, slow."

My breasts feel heavy, and my nipples tingle. I can feel myself grow wet as he somehow manages to hit me just right despite all the clothes blocking his target.

"Let me love you," he pleas as his hand finds my breast and rolls my nipple.

I groan and arch my back, pushing my chest fully into his hand. He shoves my sweater up until my bra is exposed. He wastes no time reaching around me and undoing the bra before shoving the material out of his way. Then – finally – his hands are on my naked skin.

I feel my nipples pebble into hard points as he plays with them. His mouth leaves my neck, and he lowers himself until his mouth covers my breast. I grasp his head to keep him right where he is. I feel his laughter against my skin, but I don't care. I'm not afraid to ask for what I want when I'm in bed with a man.

Bed? We're not in bed. In fact, we're in the living room with all the lights blazing. At least, Wally closed the curtains when we arrived home.

I push him away. He grunts and scowls up at me. "What's wrong now?"

"Nothing's wrong. Except my living room curtains aren't black-out curtains so anyone passing by will know exactly what we're up to."

Wally curses before bending down and shoving his shoulder into my belly.

"Bedroom it is," he says as he marches off to the bedroom with me thrown over his shoulder.

And, despite knowing allowing Wally into my bed after his big announcement is the worst idea ever, I don't stop him. I know I can. If I say the word, the man will back away. Not for long. He isn't the type of man to give up on what he wants, but he'd give me space if I demanded it.

Why then am I not demanding space to think? To figure out in my head what's going on between the two of us? I must be an idiot. Or in love. Nope. I am not thinking about the l-word right now. I refuse.

Chapter 28

Have you heard the joke about the spy? It's top secret.

Wally grunts when the doorbell rings the next evening. It's Friday, and we're both exhausted from this topsy turvy week. Was it only Monday when I discovered Flynn Price is alive and I told Wally and his brothers all my secrets? And then yesterday Wally hits me with an 'I love you'. I need a six-pack of beer and a good fight movie. The last thing I need is company.

Wally walks to the door and pulls the curtain to the side to peek outside. He drops the curtain and shakes his head before opening the door. Faith, Suzie, Phoebe, and Hailey stand on my porch smiling up at him. He sighs as he motions them inside.

"What's going on?" I ask the women.

Before they can answer, Wally kisses my forehead and whispers, "I'll be outside doing rounds. Don't do anything stupid."

"You mean like tell you not to do anything stupid?"

He flinches. "Point taken. Call if you see anything suspicious."

I push him away. "Yeah, yeah, whatever."

No one says a word as Wally dons his coat and boots before disappearing into the night. As soon as the door shuts on him, four women's gazes zero in on me. Uh oh.

"Where's Valerie?" I ask in an attempt to stall them.

"She's working."

I latch onto Faith's answer. "Working? I thought she lived in Saint Louis and was just visiting temporarily."

Faith shrugs. "I don't know what's going on with her, and she's being evasive."

Suzie slashes a hand in the air. "We'll discuss Valerie and her secrets another day. Tonight is for finding out what's going on with Chrissie."

Phoebe groans. "I thought we were here to bake Christmas cookies. Baby Rossi is hungry." She rubs her belly – her protruding belly.

Faith squeals before rushing over to hug her. "Your belly popped."

Phoebe groans. "Have you seen the size of my husband? I feel like I'm carrying a gorilla."

"Ryker is pretty hairy," Suzie says, and Hailey slaps her upside the head. "Oi, you can't hit a pregnant woman. It's a hate crime."

Hailey sighs. "You don't even bother trying to use the correct terminology, do you?"

"I don't have the ingredients for cookies," I say before Suzie can respond to Hailey.

It's not like I'm opposed to cookies and sugar, but I don't keep the stuff in my house. It's too tempting. I may have tons of discipline to go jogging and work out every day, but stay away from sugary sweets? It ain't happening.

Hailey indicates her ever-present messenger bag. "I got you covered."

I trail her as she walks into the kitchen and empties her bag. She removes flour, baking soda, baking powder, and vanilla. "I figured you'd have butter, sugar, and eggs."

I do, but only because Wally has been staying here. I know better than to say anything about my current sleeping arrangements, though. Talk about waving a red flag in front of a bull. I nod and start gathering the ingredients together.

"And I brought all kinds of fun stuff to decorate the cookies with." Faith sets Santa and Christmas tree shaped cookie cutters, green and red sprinkles, a couple of containers of premade frosting, red sanding sugar, and sugar snowflakes on the kitchen counter.

Phoebe snatches a container of pre-made frosting, but Faith slaps her hand, and she drops her booty.

"The frosting is for the cookies."

Phoebe pouts, "But I'm hungry."

"Do you want me to make you a sandwich?" I offer.

"I'm not hungry-hungry, I want sugar."

"I wouldn't mind a sandwich," Suzie says with her head in my refrigerator. "You sure have a lot of food in here for being a single woman. When I was single, I hardly had any food in my refrigerator."

"Yeah, Chrissie," Hailey adds as she peers over Suzie's shoulder to peruse my refrigerator. "It's a lot of food for a single lady."

I place my hands on my hips and stare them down. "Do I look like the type of woman who doesn't eat?"

"You have like ten pounds of hamburger in here. And are those steaks?" Suzie rummages around in the appliance.

I place a hand on her shoulder and haul her backwards away from the refrigerator before slamming it shut. "Don't you know it's rude to go digging through someone else's possessions?"

Hailey snorts. "Don't you know better than to think we won't dig into your life until we find out what's going on?"

"What makes you think something's going on?"

She rolls her eyes. "Seriously? Our men have been taking shifts to guard you. And considering you're a badass, I figure whatever's happening is dangerous."

"And yet all of you came over here tonight?" I'm surprised their men allowed them to be in my vicinity.

Suzie huffs. "All of our men are outside circling the property."

"I think it's called doing rounds," Phoebe says around a hunk of cheese. I cock an eyebrow at her. She shrugs. "Turns out I'm hungry-hungry after all."

"We've all been where you are right now," Hailey points out to me.

"Oh yeah? Where is that?"

"In danger." I cross my arms over my chest and wait for her to explain. She doesn't make me wait long. "I had a stalker. It was a big misunderstanding. He thought I took a picture of him in a compromising position, but I didn't." She points to Phoebe. "Her husband hired Ryker to kidnap her." She points to Faith. "And she had a gang in Saint Louis after her."

Suzie raises her hand. "I was never in danger and in need of Grayson to rescue me."

Hailey snorts. "Maybe not from outside forces, Ms. Klutzy."

"I'm sorry for your troubles. I truly am. But I can't tell you what's going on." Flynn Price being alive needs to be kept under wraps as much as possible. I'm still struggling with telling Wally and his brothers.

Suzie grunts. "I told you we should have tried getting the information from our men first."

Fat lot of good it would have done them. "Sorry to disappoint, but your men don't know what's happening either."

Faith's eyes widen. "Not even Max?"

"Max knows," I give in. "But Grayson, Ryker, and Aiden are not on the list of people who need to know."

"Aiden, my detective husband, doesn't know? It must be driving him batty. Come on," Hailey pleads. "I can keep a secret. You can tell me. It would kill Aiden if I knew, and he didn't." She rubs her hands together in glee.

"Sorry, not sorry." She bats her eyelashes at me, and I snort. "I'm not Aiden. Your feminine wiles do not affect me."

She grunts before flopping down on a chair at my kitchen table.

"I can try to torture the information out of Max," Faith suggests.

"You can?"

Her shoulders fall. "No. The man is a steel trap when he wants to be."

"Then, we're back to my original plan," Suzie says. "Someone get the shot glasses. We're getting Chrissie drunk until she confesses."

"I'm in," Hailey shouts. She raises an eyebrow in challenge at me. I know she grew up with Wally and his brothers and thinks she can drink me under the table. But she's wrong.

"I don't need to know all of Chrissie's secrets," Phoebe insists. "I can respect a person's privacy. I came here to bake cookies."

Faith places a hand on her elbow and leads her to the kitchen counter. "I'll make the dough, and you can use the cookie cutters to shape them before we put them in the oven."

"Meanwhile." Suzie slams a bottle of tequila and two shot glasses on the table. Why is it always tequila?

"Where did the tequila come from?"

She wags her finger at me. "Never you mind."

"Are you sure you want to do this?" I ask Hailey.

"Are you sure?"

I motion to Suzie to pour the first shots. As soon as the glasses are full, I lift mine and salute Hailey. "May the best woman win." I down the shot and drop the glass back on the table, my eyes pinned on Hailey who does the exact same thing.

After the second shot, I decide doing shots on an empty stomach is a bad idea. I'll still win this challenge, but hangovers are a bitch and much worse when you drink with nothing to line your stomach – especially once your age starts with the number four. Getting old is not for the faint of heart.

I grab some chips and salsa out of the pantry. When I return to the kitchen table, Phoebe and Faith have joined Suzie and

Hailey and the aroma of cookies fills the air. My mouth waters. It's been forever since I had homemade sugar cookies.

"Feel like telling us what's going on yet," Hailey says with a slight slur to her speech.

"I'm good." I snack on a few chips like I have nothing to worry about. I don't. Hailey will never outdrink me.

Suzie looks back and forth between us before pouring two more shots. I raise my glass and clink it against Hailey's before throwing the liquid back. The burn of the tequila is not as prevalent this time telling me I'm on my way to being good and toasted.

"I've got ten dollars on Chrissie," Phoebe says.

"Hey!" Hailey shouts. "I was your friend first."

"What are we? In kindergarten?" Phoebe replies and Hailey grunts.

"I've known Hailey the longest, but I'm still betting on Chrissie," Suzie says.

"Me too," Faith agrees.

"I can't believe this shit." Hailey's words are definitely slurred now.

"Don't worry. They can't have a bet when there's no one to bet against." I smirk. "Because everyone's on my side."

"Another round." She tries to motion to the bottle and ends up hitting it instead. Suzie rescues it before it can fall to the ground.

The oven timer buzzes. "Cookies!" Phoebe shouts before rushing toward the oven. Faith shakes her head before following her.

I decide to take pity on Hailey. "You know you can't outdrink me. And I can't tell you what's going on."

"Can you give us a clue?" Suzie asks and taps her nose like we're in a corny spy movie. I ignore her and watch as Phoebe and Faith return carrying a tray of freshly baked cookies and all the bits to decorate them with.

"Why don't we leave Chrissie alone and decorate our cookies?" Faith suggests. "Ollie will kill me if I return home empty-handed."

Phoebe freezes. "You mean we can't eat all of these?"

"We made three dozen cookies."

Phoebe shrugs. "There are five of us. That's less than a dozen cookies each."

I hear a snore and glance across the table to find Hailey slumped over in her chair, passed out.

"I get her share of cookies," Phoebe declares as she slathers frosting on a cookie.

Suzie inches close to Hailey before giving her ear a quick, hard tug. Hailey wakes with a start. "What? What happened?"

"You passed out like a freshman at orientation week. And we acted like adults and didn't write all over your face with frosting."

Phoebe gasps before drawing the containers of frosting to her bosom. "No one's wasting the frosting with stupid pranks." She glares at everyone in warning.

"Whatever." Suzie slumps in her chair. "I guess we'll have to try a different tactic for finding out Chrissie's secrets another day."

Faith giggles. "I don't think you're supposed to warn her in advance."

"Oops!"

"Fine," I sigh. "I'll give you one hint and then you have to drop it."

Suzie crosses her heart. "Promise."

"It's about an ex."

"I knew it!" she shouts and raises her arms in victory. The action causes her chair to fall over sending her to the floor. "I'm fine!"

"We know!" Phoebe and Hailey shout in unison.

Chapter 29

What type of shoes do spies wear? Sneakers.

I GROAN AS I roll over in bed the next morning. Behind me, Wally chuckles.

"Shut up, you," I grunt at him, but the effort makes pain burst behind my eyes. Ouch!

I don't know what's worse – the headache from all the tequila or the stomachache from all the sugar. Poor Faith is going to have to make more Christmas cookies for Ollie because there are no cookies left over from last night. Actually, there were a few but then Suzie decided to give all the Santas 'proper anatomy'. No way is Faith giving Ollie pornographic cookies.

"I'm all for you drinking a bucketload of tequila before decorating yourself with frosting as long as I get to shower with you afterwards."

I groan. He's not exaggerating. I did paint my face with frosting and sprinkles. Thankfully, I wasn't the only one. By the time Ryker, Aiden, Max, and Grayson arrived to pick up their better halves last night, all of us were 'decorated'. I don't know what Phoebe and Suzie's excuse is, but I'm blaming the tequila.

I have other excuses as well. My behavior last night might have had something to do with how it was the first time I've spent the evening with girlfriends since I was in college. It's been such a long time since I had girlfriends to do silly things with, I may have allowed things to get a bit out of control.

I cover my head with a pillow. "The kitchen is probably a disaster area."

Wally climbs on top of me before snatching the pillow away. "Do you think I'd let you wake up to a dirty house?"

"Duh. It's my mess to clean up."

He kisses my nose. "Angel, it's handled."

"When?"

Seriously, when did he have time to clean the kitchen? After my friends left last night, he dragged me into the shower where he cleaned me up before doing dirty things to me, and then we crashed in bed.

He smiles before giving me a quick, closed lip kiss. He rolls off me and out of the bed before grabbing my hand. "Come on. I'll make you breakfast. It'll make you feel better."

I grab hold of his hand, and he helps me to stand. My knees are shaky, but I actually don't feel as bad as I expected to feel this morning when Hailey started her whole 'I'm going to drink you under the table'-thing. I stretch my neck from side to side as I evaluate how my muscles are doing.

"I think I'll go for my run before I eat."

Wally's hand spasms in mine. "Why don't you run on the treadmill at the gym until we find Price?"

"I need the fresh air."

"It's freezing out there."

"It's nearly forty degrees."

"There's snow on the ground."

I pull back the curtain on the window. "Huh. It must be invisible snow." Thursday's early snowfall melted by Friday afternoon. "Next excuse."

He wraps his arm around my waist and pulls me away from the window. "We can do our own exercise inside."

He licks my neck, and I'm tempted. Very, very tempted. But I need to get a run in. I have too much nervous energy coursing through my body with everything that's happened this week. The only way to expend it is a nice, long run.

"Why don't you come with me?" I suggest. As if he'd let me go alone anyway. "I'll let you wash me off afterwards." I waggle my eyebrows.

Wally grunts. "Fine. We'll go for a run."

Despite claiming it's not too cold out, I bundle myself up. I put on my thermal tights and top before donning a light jacket. When I reach for my earbuds, Wally growls. "No."

I raise my hands in surrender. "Sorry. Habit."

I know better than to listen to music when someone's hunting me. I usually only put in one earbud, but I need to be one-hundred percent alert with Flynn out there. He's not usually a morning person, but he is the person who will do absolutely anything to get what he wants. And apparently what he wants right now is to capture me. Asshole.

"You ready? Did you call in back-up?"

He cocks an eyebrow but doesn't otherwise respond.

"You called in back-up," I mutter as I disengage the alarm.

I open the door and a blast of cold wind from Lake Michigan hits me. Maybe this wasn't the best idea after all. I inhale a deep breath and as I exhale, I force all the negative thoughts from me. I do a few stretches on the porch before starting toward the park.

As I jog, I remain aware and alert of my surroundings. I notice Wally falling back. I'm surprised he's willing to make me vulnerable again, but then I spot Barney and Lenny stretching on a bench when I enter the park.

I begin the one-mile loop around the park. One section of the loop is wooded. If Flynn is going to come after me this morning, this is where he'll be. I slow as I make my way through the woods, practically daring the asshole to come after me, but nothing happens.

When I return to the open stretch of the park where the benches and playground are, Barney and Lenny are no longer there. I glance around and notice Barney at the beginning of the wooded section and Lenny at the end. I would bet good money Wally is somewhere in the trees hiding.

I quicken my speed through the open area but slow down once I reach the woods again. I don't spot Wally, but I can feel his eyes on mine. Flynn will never see him coming, assuming Flynn is going to make his move this morning.

I sigh in disappointment when I exit the woods. Looks like Flynn is a no-show for 'the capture Chrissie on her run'-show.

I'm sprinting toward the end of my second loop when some-one jumps out from behind the bench and tackles me. I spin as we fall to make sure I land on top of him. Him being Flynn. Of course, it is. He knew exactly what we were thinking. He let everyone gather around the wooded area and came at me when I was vulnerable and exposed.

With Flynn's arms wound around me, I don't have my hands free to fight him. Good thing I don't need my hands to fight. Using my core strength, I slam the top of my head into his nose. Blood spurts forth and drenches my top as I hear the crunch of his nose breaking.

"Bitch."

He rolls us, but there's no way I'm letting him get the upper hand by being on top of me. It's bad enough my arms are pinned. Lucky for me, my legs are free. I wrap my legs around him to hinder his movement. His arms loosen around me, and I know I'll have mere seconds to attack while I've got an opening.

I don't get my moment. Wally comes charging at us at top speed and grabs Flynn by the back of his jacket before throwing him off of me. I jump to my feet, but before I can catch my balance, Wally has Flynn pinned to the ground, his hands behind his back.

Lenny appears and slaps a pair of flexicuffs on Flynn's wrists. Wally drags Flynn to his feet by the cuffs – an action I know to be extremely painful.

"Time to talk, Price."

"I'm not telling you shit."

Wally grins. "Good. This is going to be fun."

A truck screeches to a halt next to the park. I look over as the door swings open and Max appears. "We need to get out of here before someone calls it in."

I search the area and notice a few parents at the playground with their phones out. I smile and wave at them, but considering I'm covered in Flynn's blood, I don't think I'm calming them down any. Oh well.

I follow behind Wally as he frog marches Flynn to the truck flanked by Lenny and Barney. No one's taking any chances.

Wally notices me behind him and opens his mouth. I don't let him speak. "If whatever you're going to say is about me staying behind, you can save your breath. I'm going with."

"She always was a stubborn bitch," Flynn says.

Wally grabs his hair and pulls his face around until he's glaring down at him. "I'd keep my mouth shut if I were you."

Flynn rolls his eyes. "Or what? You're going to kill me? You don't have it in you."

Wally smirks while his brothers laugh. "I told you this was going to be fun."

I climb into the front seat while Wally, Lenny, and Barney squeeze into the back.

When Max pulls into the street, I comment, "I knew my membership in the wholesale store would come in handy. I'm all stocked up on garbage bags and industrial cleaning solutions."

Everyone chuckles and the fear of their judgment I've been holding onto seeps out of my body. These men aren't going to condemn me for going rogue. If they did, they wouldn't be here. I let all of my concerns about their opinions go as Max drives us to Wally's house.

Chapter 30

What do you call a cow spying on another cow? A steak out.

Max drives past Wally's house and around the block to the alley behind it. He turns into the alley and pulls up behind a shed in Wally's backyard. It feels like these men have done this before, but I'm not going to ask. Their secrets are their secrets. I know how difficult it is when secrets become common knowledge.

Sid is standing in front of the shed with his arms crossed over his chest scanning the area. When Max switches off the engine, he lifts his chin signaling the area is clear.

I exit the vehicle and keep guard as Wally escorts Flynn into the shed. I scan the inside as Wally secures Flynn to a chair. It's practically empty except for a few garden utensils hanging on the walls. Does Wally interrogate people here more often? I can't stop myself from checking the floor for bloodstains.

Wally comes to stand beside me as we watch Flynn glare at us.

"Am I supposed to be impressed with your new boyfriend?" Flynn snarls.

"Damn," Barney mumbles before removing his wallet and slapping a twenty-dollar bill in Lenny's hand. "Some double agent you are. You started running your mouth within seconds."

"Told you," Lenny says.

"I'm not telling you shit," Flynn insists.

"Good thing we don't want to know shit." Wally advances until he's standing within arm's reach of Flynn. "We want to know why you're after Chrissie."

"Chrissie?" Flynn snorts. "Lindberg certainly has you wrapped around her little finger."

I lock my body to stop myself from flinching at his words. How could I forget his refusal to use my first name? Even when we were intimate, he never used my name. He called me babe or some other vague endearment.

I'm such an idiot. Why the hell did I sacrifice my career for this jerk? Was I so desperate for someone to notice me, to love me, that I ignored all the red flags?

"You can't seriously believe Chrissie is a good person. Haven't you read her file? She's been disavowed."

Good thing my muscles are locked up tight because otherwise, those words would have caused the flinch of all flinches. What an asshole! I was disavowed because I went against orders to save his ass. When it came out Flynn was a double agent, no one trusted me anymore. Not only had I been dating the man, but I went all out to find him when I thought he was captured. Captured? Snort.

"Oh yeah? Tell me more," Wally coaxes.

At Wally's words, Sid pats my back where Flynn can't see. It's sweet he thinks I need comfort. I don't. I trust Wally, which is infinitely scarier than listening to him interrogate Flynn Price.

Flynn grins, thinking he's got Wally now. Geez. Is this guy seriously a double agent? He sucks at being interrogated. Did he skip class the week we did extensive training to prepare for the various interrogation methods?

"Haven't you heard? She's suspected of working for the Russians."

Max snorts, and Wally glares at him. "Sorry, brother. I couldn't help myself. This guy is an embarrassment to the agency."

Flynn flinches, and it suddenly all makes sense. I shove Wally out of the way so I can stand in front of Flynn. Wally tries to pull me away, but I ignore him.

"That's why you started selling secrets, isn't it? They were getting ready to let you go."

He scowls. "They were putting me on recruitment duty. Recruitment duty!"

Recruitment duty is one station up from a desk. It's also a tried and true method to 'retire' an agent from the field. Unlike the movies would have everyone believe, the agency doesn't kill agents once they're no longer useful.

I smirk. "And now the Russians figured out you were no longer useful to them."

It's all beginning to make sense to me now. I've been racking my brain trying to figure out why Flynn would come after me now. The entire US government assumed he was dead. He could live his years out in Russia without ever having to worry about anyone coming after him. Only he couldn't live in Russia because they didn't want him anymore when he became useless.

"And now you've come after me for revenge?"

"You ruined my life!" Spittle flies from his mouth as he shouts. "If it weren't for you, I could have continued to butter my bread on both sides."

I wag my finger at him. "Nuh-uh. Recruitment duty, remember?"

He slumps into the chair. Not much. Wally secured him pretty tight after all. "Do what you're going to do to me."

"We're not going to do anything."

"Hey! Wait a minute! I thought we'd at least slap him around a bit," Barney protests.

Lenny cracks his knuckles. "Screw slapping him around. I want to get a few punches in."

Wally growls in agreement, and I pat his arm to calm him. "I'm going to step outside and call Cruz. The phone call may take a while, and who knows how long it will be before his team arrives so we can hand this piece of shit off?"

"You cold-hearted bitch!" Flynn shouts. "You're going to let them lock me up in a dark hole somewhere. You love me!"

"Dude, I never loved you. I must have been temporarily insane to ever think I ever did."

My eyes find Wally's. Now that I know what love feels like, I know what I had with Flynn was definitely not love. I don't think I even liked the guy to be honest. I was lonely and he knew how to manipulate my loneliness. He may suck as an agent, but he's not an idiot when it comes to using women.

But Wally? There's a man who's easy to love. He would stand between me and any danger coming my way. Hell, he has done exactly that. Holy crap on a cracker. Do I love him?

Wally trails a finger down my face. Judging by the warmth in his eyes, he knows exactly what I'm thinking. Lucky for me, there's no time for the l-word conversation right now.

"Go make your call. We promise not to hurt him too much."

I wave my hand. "Like I care. Have at it."

I exit the shed, shutting the door securely behind me. I hear the sound of flesh hitting flesh and keep walking until I'm on the other side of the yard. I don't care what's going on behind the closed door right now, but I don't think Wally wants me to hear.

I pull out my phone and dial Deputy Director Cruz's private line.

"Lindberg," he grunts when he answers.

"I need to arrange a pick-up."

"Location?"

I give him the coordinates for Wally's shed. I'm about to disconnect the phone –there's nothing more to say to the man who accused me of being a traitor after all – when Cruz speaks.

"I can make your past disappear if you want to come back."

I still. I've waited over a year to hear those words, but those words don't fill me with the joy I once expected them to. All I feel now is trepidation. The company had no problem turning their backs on me once. What's to say they won't do it again?

"Why would I want to come back?"

"Because we need you."

Damn him. Those are the very words used to convince me to abandon my chosen career path after college. I had planned to join the police force after obtaining my degree in criminal justice, but then the Khobar Towers bombing happened.

I thought by joining the agency I could combat terrorism like the bombing in Saudi Arabia that killed nineteen U.S. Air Force personnel and make the world a safer place to live in. And I did manage to stop several terrorist attacks. But I'm not ready to return to the shadows. Not when I've found my light.

"I think it's time to make my retirement permanent."

"All I ask is you think about it," Cruz pushes because the man can't stop himself.

"I will," I say, although I have no plans to seriously consider returning.

"Pick up is three minutes out," he says and hangs up.

I return my phone to my pocket before heading back to the shed to tell the brothers their fun is over.

Chapter 31

What do you call a frog spy? A croak and dagger agent.

WALLY TUGS ME TOWARD the entrance to McGraw's Pub while I drag my feet. It's Saturday night of the never-ending week. I'm tired and grumpy and not in the mood to deal with a bunch of people. Other than Wally. I can deal with him all day and night long. Damnit. Where did those thoughts come from?

"Come on. You need food after the day you've had."

"We can order in and eat naked in bed." I waggle my eyebrows at him.

"You're topped up. You should be good for a few hours."

He's not lying. He got down on his knees in the shower and his mouth did magical things to me before he hauled me out of the shower and threw me on my bed where he proceeded to show me his age hasn't affected his stamina one dang bit.

He swings the door open, and everyone shouts 'Surprise!' I whirl on Wally. "Is it your birthday and you didn't tell me?"

He chuckles. "No, Angel. They're here for you."

"It's not my birthday."

"I know, Angel. We're celebrating your safety."

"This is completely unnecessary," I grump to hide how overwhelmed I am to have people in my life who are grateful I'm alive.

He rubs his nose along mine. "It is necessary. I love you, Angel."

My chest contracts at his words as warmth flows through me. I don't think I'll ever get used to hearing those words. I don't want to.

"Okay," I concede. "We can stay for an hour."

Wally's head descends, but before his lips can meet mine, Suzie asks, "Can we have her now?"

He squeezes my shoulder before sauntering off to join his brothers at their standard booth. Suzie snatches my hand and pulls me to the bar where Phoebe, Hailey, Valerie, and some woman I don't know are congregating.

"This is Aunt Mary Ann. She's married to Uncle Sid."

I smile in greeting at the woman. She's nearly as tall as me but unlike me, she has olive skin and dark, curly hair.

"I'm sorry we haven't met before. I'm an ER nurse and work erratic hours."

Suzie bumps her shoulder. "Plus, Sid keeps her tied to the bed when she's off."

Mary Ann's cheeks darken. "It's true."

Faith forces her way past the women and wraps her arms around me. "I'm glad you're safe now." With the way she clings to me, I have a feeling she knows more about what happened, but I don't question her. If Max trusts her, then I'm trusting Max.

"I wasn't ever in much danger."

"Dude, you literally have a bruise the size of a fist on your forehead right now", Suzie points out.

I resist the urge to touch the area. It'll only encourage her. Besides, it's not from a fist. This bruise is all thanks to my headbutting Flynn. The man's head is freaking hard.

"Now, can you tell us what happened?" Suzie says and bats her eyelashes at me.

"Nope," I say popping the P since I know it drives her crazy.

"All I know is Aiden got a call this morning telling him to keep patrol vehicles away from the park near Chrissie's house," Hailey says before asking me, "Do you want to explain?"

"This is the first I've heard about it." I'm not lying. I didn't know anyone called Aiden. I'm not surprised, but I technically have no prior knowledge of the call.

Hailey crosses her arms over her chest and harrumphs. "Do you have any idea what it cost me to get that tiny bit of information? Help a sister out."

Phoebe rolls her eyes. "Oh, please. Like we don't know you enjoyed every single second of whatever you had to do to get Aiden to talk."

Hailey bites her lip. "It was fun."

Suzie growls. "This is not helping any."

Time to end this. I grasp her shoulders. She huffs and I give her the look until she calms down. "Suzie, I like you. I consider you a friend, which is a big deal in my life." She opens her mouth, but I squeeze her shoulders to stop her from speaking. "But I'm not going to tell you what happened. Ever. You're going to have to learn to live with not knowing." She sighs. "If it makes you feel better, you can make up some crazy story."

Her eyes light up. "Can I tell people the story I make up and act like it's the truth and I am the only one who knows the truth because we're such good friends?"

"Go for it." It's not like anyone's going to believe any cockamamie story she makes up anyway.

"This goes for all of you," I order the group of women. "I will never tell you what happened. Not because I don't consider you friends or don't trust you, but because I can't."

Phoebe doesn't hesitate to nod. "Secrets are best buried." She would know.

"I need to get out more often. I have no idea what's going on, but I'm thoroughly intrigued." When I frown at Mary Ann, she holds up her hands. "Don't worry. I'm good with secrets. You wouldn't believe some of the shit I witness in the ER." Suzie rubs her hands together. "But I can't tell you." Suzie deflates.

"Now, we've got Chrissie settled, it's time to check out what Wally's up to." Hailey points to the table where Wally, Barney, Sid, and Lenny are sitting.

"What do you mean?" Mary Ann asks.

"You'll see," Hailey sings as she walks to a standing table within hearing range of the brothers. We all follow. I have a feeling it's prank time. It's been a while since any pranking happened thanks to my stalker issue.

The door opens and three men who could be models enter. Before I can blink, Ryker, Grayson, Aiden, and Max are at our table with their arms around their women. I'm surprised they're not barking and snarling at the men.

I catch Wally's eye and cock an eyebrow. He winks at me. Looks like I know who will be doing the pranking today.

The three men don't hesitate to approach the table where the brothers are sitting. Sid and Barney look confused, Lenny looks interested, and Wally looks amused.

"Shit," Max mutters under his breath.

One of the men bends over and whispers something in Sid's ear. Sid jumps to his feet and points at Wally. "You asshole! My wife is here."

I glance over my shoulder at his wife. Mary Ann is bent over holding her stomach while tears of laughter roll down her face.

Sid stomps to her and places a hand on her back. "Come on. We're leaving."

"No way, mister. I'm staying."

He sighs and wraps an arm around her and places her in front of him as if protecting himself from the man who approached him. The man who can't keep his eyes off of him.

Valerie marches to the table and slams a hand down on it in front of Barney. "You could have just told me you're not interested in me. You didn't have to throw a date in my face."

She spins around and rushes off toward the restrooms. Barney chases after her. "I'm not interested in men," he yells.

Lenny waggles his eyebrows at the men surrounding the table. "I'm interested in men."

The three men look at each other before they each shrug. Lenny stands. "Later." He waves as he leads the men out of the bar.

Phoebe's jaw is on the floor. "Did Lenny just pick up three men at once?"

"You better not be thinking about what you can do with three men all at the same time," Ryker grumbles.

Her eyes widen. "I wasn't. But now I am." She pauses. "I don't get it. There's not enough…" She trails off as her face flames. "Never mind."

"Yeah, yeah, Lenny's a man whore, but what's going on with Valerie and Barney?" Suzie's eyes are aimed at the hallway leading to the restrooms. "Let's go eavesdrop."

Grayson grabs her hand before she can move. "No."

She sticks out her bottom lip and pouts. "But—"

"Behave."

Wally stands behind me, and I lean into him. "Why didn't you tell me beforehand? I wouldn't have whined about coming had I known."

"It was more fun to witness your surprise."

I admit it would have ruined the surprise had I known about it beforehand. "But you didn't get Max," I point out.

"I'm not an idiot. I can't sleep with one eye open for the rest of my life."

Max smirks. "Glad you finally figured out you can't best me, brother."

Wally scoffs. "I can best you, but I know better than to get between you and Faith."

In response, Max tightens his arm around Faith.

Wally kisses the side of my head. "Glad you came out?"

I glance around the table filled with my friends, their partners, and Wally's brothers. The sight of these people who took me in and befriended me with hardly any questions asked warms my heart. It's taken me thirty years since my parents passed, but I think I finally found my home.

Chapter 32

What do you call a spy programmer? Commando.

THE MOMENT I CLOSE the door behind me, Wally backs me up against the wall. His lips meet mine, and he fists my ponytail to tilt my head to where he wants it. I snarl and fight back a little. Not because I don't like the feel of his lips on mine or his hand fisting my hair – I do – but I can't allow him to be the boss of me all the time.

He bites my bottom lip in punishment. "Don't fight me."

"I'll fight you if I want, Bossy."

He bends his knees and rocks his hips. At the feel of his hardness rubbing my center, my mouth opens in a moan, and his tongue dashes inside to plunder. I dig my fingernails into his shoulders, and he groans down my throat.

I touch my tongue to his and try to force him out of my mouth. Our tongues end up dueling as he continues to grind into my core.

I wrench my mouth from his and let my head fall back against the wall. "Feels good." I wrap a leg around his hip to gain leverage to rub myself up and down his hardness.

His hands move to my hips, and he lifts me. I don't hesitate to wrap my legs around his hips. "Bed or couch?"

"Couch. There's no reason for you to stay the night."

Wally's lips, which had been licking their way across my neck, stop. "What did you say?"

"There's no reason for you to stay the night," I repeat.

He glares at me before loosening his arms until I have to climb down or risk falling on my ass. I sigh. I was hoping to have this conversation after our sexy times.

"What's the big deal? You know you don't have to stay here anymore. My stalker is caught. I'm perfectly safe."

A muscle in his jaw clenches. "Do you think the only reason I'm here is because of your stalker?"

It sounds like a rhetorical question, so I don't answer.

"Do you?" he hisses.

I guess it wasn't a rhetorical question.

"No."

He nods. "Do you believe me when I say I love you?"

Geez. Get right to the heart of the matter why don't you? "I do."

He places a hand against my cheek. "Can you say it like you mean it?"

I throw my hands in the air. "Can't we slow down for a minute? You told me you loved me …" I count the days on my fingers. Thursday night, Friday, Saturday night. "Three days ago."

"I told you. I want what I want."

"I understand. It's not lost on me the kind of man you are, but can you consider me for a minute?"

His nostrils flare. "You're all I consider."

Ugh. "I didn't mean you aren't considerate with me. You are. You're an absolute gentleman."

He smirks. "Except in bed."

"Yeah, yeah. Except in bed." He advances on me, but I retreat. He scowls.

"No, you don't get to scowl. Think about it for a minute. I've had no one, no family, hardly any friends for decades. All I've had is one traitorous boyfriend. And yet, here you are forcing your way into my life within two months of meeting me. You even moved your clothes into my closet without telling me."

"You caught that, did you?"

I point to myself. "Spy, remember?" Former spy technically, although my old job is there for the taking should I wish it.

Wally runs a hand down his face. "I thought if I moved in here and showed you how good we are together, you'd be less hesitant about us."

"No, you thought you'd move in here without telling me, and then when I realized what was happening, I'd accept us living together since we already were."

He doesn't bother to contradict me. He can't. I know I'm right.

"Haven't you enjoyed having me here every night this past week?"

"I have, but do you hear yourself? It's been a week."

"Angel, I'm too old for this dating crap. I love you, I want to be with you, I'm pulling out all the stops to make it happen."

He certainly is.

"It's too quick. It's too fast." I clutch my stomach. It's rolling with all the emotions flowing through my body right now.

Wally cocks his head and studies me for a moment before taking my hand and leading me to the sofa. He settles me on his lap and cups my cheeks with his hands.

"Angel, it's time for you to admit you love me."

Tell him I love him? I push against his chest and try to climb to my feet. He clamps his arms around me and holds me right where I am. I know I can escape, but I'll have to hurt him to do so and the last thing in the world I want to do is hurt Wally.

I only admitted to myself I love Wally this morning. I'm not ready to crack open my bruised heart and hand it to him. It's too soon. I know I sound like a broken record, but it's the truth.

"It's not too soon," Wally says proving he can read my mind.

"It is," I continue to insist.

"Angel, you know as well as I do how precious life is. It can be over in a blink of an eye. There are no guarantees for tomorrow." His eyes fill with pain and regrets before he blinks and it vanishes. I know him showing me his suffering is a gift. A gift I should know better than to squander.

"I'm not going to wait an arbitrary time period before society finds it acceptable for me to declare my love. Fuck that. And there's no reason for you to hold back either. After having Price stalking you all week, trying to end you, I'd hoped you felt the same way."

"Are you trying to guilt-trip me into admitting I love you?"

His smile stretches from ear to ear. "Admitting you love me?"

Hell and damnation. He's good. He got me to say I love you without saying I love you. But there are things we need to discuss before the actual three little words will pass my lips for real.

"What about your job? I don't think I can handle being with someone who still plays in the shadows."

I'm not lying or pushing him away. After everything I endured with Flynn, I'm not feeling very confident about dating someone still working with the agency.

Wally tucks a stray strand of hair behind my ear. "I'm retired."

This is news to me. "Since when?"

"Since Tuesday when I called Deputy Director Cruz and told him I was done as soon as we found Price."

"This isn't what I want. I don't want you to retire for me. I don't want you to live with regrets."

"I'm not retiring for you, although I would if you asked." He pauses and waits for a reaction to his statement, but I keep my mouth clamped shut. "I'm retiring because it's time. I'm fifty-nine years old and I've been working for our government in some compacity for nearly forty years. I could use a rest."

"But what are you going to do with your time?"

Wally doesn't seem like the type of man to hang around at McGraw's Pub all day and night like the rest of his brothers.

"Woodworking." My eyes widen, and he chuckles. "You didn't think my shed was just for interrogating terrorists, did you?"

To be honest, I wondered. "It was pretty empty. I didn't detect any woodworking tools." He whistles and gazes up at the ceiling. "You didn't!" He better not have. "Where did you put them?"

"They're not here. I've only packed them up thus far. I want to build a shed in your backyard first."

My stomach heaves. "You're going to build a shed in my backyard!"

"I'm not doing the woodworking in the garage. I want you to have somewhere to park your car in the winter. I won't have you getting into a cold vehicle every morning."

I slap his shoulder. "You're infuriating." How can he turn him wanting to force his way into my life by building a shed in *my* backward into a sweet gesture?

"Get used to it. I'm always going to make sure you're taken care of first and foremost." He kisses my forehead. "What about you? Are you going back to the agency?"

I jolt. "How did you know?"

"Cruz called me. He asked me to help persuade you to return."

The ass! "He better not have. I told him I wasn't interested, but he insisted I think about it."

"And? Have you thought about it?"

"When did I have the time? He literally asked me this morning." It's not like I've had any time alone since then. Wally must have snuck off to talk to Cruz while I was in the bathroom since he's been my shadow the whole day.

"Stop stalling."

I give in. After all, I know my answer. "I'm not going back. I don't want to work for people who can turn their backs on you as easily as they did to me."

Wally squeezes my neck. "What are you going to do? Working as an office manager is going to bore you."

"I know. I'm surprised I've lasted this long. Sitting behind a desk is not my thing. I'm thinking of getting my PI license. It's too late for me to join the police force but being a private investigator would be similar."

I know, I know. I initially said I wasn't interested in becoming a PI, but I'm done lying to myself about being okay with working as an office manager.

"You'll make a great PI."

I grin. "Of course, I will. I've got skills."

"You done with your excuses now?"

I widen my eyes, but I don't bat my eyelashes. It would be a step too far. "What do you mean?"

"Don't give me your innocent act."

Now, I do bat my eyelashes. "I thought I was an angel."

"You're a pain in my ass is what you are."

I wink. "And damn proud of it, too."

"Rip off the bandage. The first time is the most difficult, but it'll get easier."

I groan. "Can't we acknowledge we both agree how I feel about you without me saying the words?"

"Not happening. I'm not settling for anything less than the woman I love telling me she loves me."

"You're annoying."

"And you love me."

I sigh. "Yeah, I do."

He cups his ear. "What did you say?"

I snap my teeth at him. "I love you, Mr. Bossy. Are you happy now?"

"Ecstatic," he murmurs before his lips find mine, and he proceeds to show me precisely how happy he is.

Chapter 33

What do you call a Dutch spy who specializes in chemical warfare? Agent Orange.

WALLY

I groan when Chrissie wiggles her ass against me as we lay in bed on Sunday morning.

"Stop it or we'll never get out of bed," I grumble in her ear.

"I'm down with that plan," she says and wiggles her ass against me again. My cock hardens at the feel of her curves cradled against me. She feels it and giggles.

"As much as I'd love to accept what you're offering, we haven't got time."

She glances over her shoulder at me. "Why not? It's Sunday morning. I don't have to work. You announced your retirement last night. What's the rush?"

I kiss her nose. "It's Christmas Eve tonight and we haven't decorated our tree yet."

"Because I've had lots and lots of time on my hands."

I brush the hair out of her face. "I'm not criticizing." I kiss her nose again to reassure her. "But our tree could give Charlie Brown a run for his money for ugliest little tree."

"I'm more of a Lucy fan myself."

I grin. "I bet you are. You probably love it when she pulls the football away from him."

Her smile is wide. "And he falls for it every dang time."

I tickle her ribs until she's giggling and gasping for breath. "Stop it! I'm going to pee my pants."

I trace her skin from her ribs to her hips. "Looks like you're not wearing any pants or underpants."

"Underpants?" She makes a face. "How old are you?"

"I'll show you how old I am." I rock my hard cock into her.

She moans and wraps her legs around me. "I dare you."

I check the alarm clock. It's not yet ten a.m. The mall's open until five. I guess we've got time.

It's nearly noon by the time we enter the mall. The place is packed with frantic shoppers buying last minute Christmas presents. Chrissie's presents are already purchased and ready to be put under the tree. She's going to freak out when she opens them. I can't wait.

Chrissie frowns as she surveys the crowds. "I should have bought Christmas tree decorations online."

"I'm glad you didn't."

Her brow wrinkles. "Why? Then, we wouldn't be here right now."

I cradle her face with my hands. "Because this is your first Christmas in a long time. I want to enjoy every aspect of it with you, even if it's fighting frantic shoppers in the mall on Christmas Eve."

Her eyes warm and she falls into me. I gladly accept her weight. I will always support her. She may have admitted she loves me yesterday, but I know we have a long way to go before she trusts in her own feelings. And I'll keep pushing her the entire time.

"Where did super-secret agent Wally go?"

I kiss her forehead. "He retired to spend more time with the love of his life with whom he lives."

Her eyes narrow. "We never finished our discussion about you moving in with me last night."

Because I distracted her in ways we both enjoyed. There's no way Chrissie is going to agree to my moving in without a fight. Thus, distraction.

I wink at her. "If we live together, I can wake you up every morning like I did this morning."

She throws her arms up in the air. "You're infuriating."

I grasp her hand and lead her toward a department store. "Come on. Let's buy some decorations for our poor tree."

"*My* poor tree," she mutters under her breath. I pretend not to hear her.

When we find the Christmas decorations section, Chrissie comes to a screeching halt. Her eyes widen as she observes the chaos.

"I've seen lions fight over the carcass of a gazelle not twenty feet from me. This is scarier." She shivers.

I place my hand on the small of her back and force her forward. "Don't tell me Chrissie is scared."

"I'm not scared. I'm cautious." She straightens her shoulders. "Okay. We need lights, garland, and ornaments."

"What about tinsel?"

She shakes her head. "Not environmentally sound. It's made of plastic, and you can't re-use it."

"Shall we divide and conquer?"

"I'll—" My words are cut off when someone shoves into us from behind. I turn around to confront whoever it is, but they've already rushed onward toward the toy department.

I take Chrissie's hand. "No. We stick together."

We wade into the crowd. There aren't many holiday decorations left, and the shoppers are picking over the remaining items like scavengers.

"Here's garland," Chrissie says and picks up the last package of garland.

A woman beside her screeches. "That's mine!"

Chrissie cocks her head. "I believe I was here first," she says in a calm voice, which merely serves to infuriate the woman.

"I saw it first!"

Chrissie snorts. "Yeah, no. Seeing doesn't confer ownership." She starts to walk away, but the woman stands to block her.

"I have pepper spray and I'm not afraid to use it."

Chrissie laughs. "You do realize we're in a crowded indoor environment. If you use pepper spray, you'll end up getting as big a dose of it as I do."

The woman sticks her hand into her bag, and I try to push Chrissie out of the way. She doesn't let me. She winks up at me. "I got this."

I know she does, but I don't want her to have to deal with a crazy shopper. This is supposed to be our first Christmas outing together. I'm building memories here, and this stranger is ruining them.

As the woman rummages in the bag, Chrissie pulls her sweater up and hitches it over her holster displaying her handgun. The woman mumbles, "Hold on. It's in here somewhere."

Chrissie is shaking with silent laughter now. "You want me to wait here until you find your pepper spray and then you'll spray me?"

The woman frowns as she finally stops digging in her purse and spots Chrissie's gun for the first time. Her jaw drops open before she purses her lips. "Fine. I guess it's your garland."

The woman stomps away and Chrissie bursts into laughter. She covers her weapon with her sweater again. "You're right. This is fun."

Only my Chrissie would think it's fun to scare the snot out of a fellow shopper on Christmas Eve. Damn, I love her.

She points to a display. "Let's grab the lights next."

We choose multi-colored light strands and Chrissie places the box in her basket. I snatch the basket from her.

"I can carry my own shopping basket."

I kiss her hair. "I know you can, but you don't have to."

"Stop being sweet," she grumbles as she marches off to find ornaments.

When we reach the aisle with Christmas ornaments, it's jam packed with shoppers. Chrissie's eyes light up at the sight.

"I thought you didn't like busy stores."

"That was before I realized people carry pepper spray and get dumb about the most stupid things."

I tug on her ponytail. "You're hoping for a brawl, aren't you?"

She shrugs. "Maybe."

I motion her forward. "Have at it, Angel."

"Which reminds me. We need an angel for the top of the tree." She scans the area until she finds what she wants. "There. It's perfect."

She shoves her way through the mass of people until she comes to the shelf with the angel she wants. There's only one left and as she reaches for it, a woman elbows her out of the way to grab for the box. Before the woman can touch the box, Chrissie has her arm pinned behind her back.

"Are you trying to steal my angel?" she snaps at her.

The woman, obviously not realizing the danger she's in, snarls in Chrissie's face. "It's mine. I saw it first."

Chrissie sighs. "What is it with the whole 'I saw it first'-thing? Is this some unwritten shopping mall rule I should know about?" she asks me.

I don't bother answering. Instead, I remove the box from the shelf and put it in our basket. The woman doesn't notice me as Chrissie lectures her on proper shopping etiquette.

"And," she finishes up, "you never elbow anyone in an unknown situation." She lifts her sweater with one hand to show her weapon. "Because you never know who you're dealing with. I could be a violent person for all you know."

I chuckle. She literally has the woman's arm pinned while lecturing her and she thinks she's non-violent.

"Baby," I call. "We need to get ornaments before we leave."

Chrissie releases the woman. "On my way." She spins around and marches away without a second glance at the woman. The woman who is now staring at Chrissie like she just met her first mass murderer.

I wrap an arm around her as I maneuver us through the crowd to the display of ornaments. Chrissie freezes next to me.

"What is it now?" I ask her.

She points to a woman. "She just shoved a box down the front of her pants," she explains before marching forward to stand in front of the woman.

She holds out her hand. "Hand it over."

The woman's eyes widen and her bottom lip trembles. "You're not wearing the store uniform."

Chrissie wiggles her fingers. "Come on. Give it up. I'm not letting you leave here with stolen goods down your pants."

The woman leans forward and whispers to Chrissie, "But it's the last Snoopy ornament."

"I don't care if it is the last Snoopy ornament. It's stealing."

At Chrissie's pronouncement, the other shoppers stop their pawing through the boxes and turn to her. Son of a bitch. I move to stand next to Chrissie, but the crowd is converging on her and I can't get through.

"The last Snoopy ornament."

"She has the last one."

"Not if I can help it."

I start grabbing women by their coats and shoving them out of the way. By the time I reach Chrissie, she's standing on top of the display rack holding the ornament high above her.

"What is wrong with you people?" she asks. She glares at them until the murmuring quiets down.

"Do you want to spend Christmas in the hospital with broken bones because of a Christmas ornament?" A few people mutter a response, but she glares at them again and they shut right up. "It was a rhetorical question."

Chrissie points at me. "Go ask management to check whether they have anymore of these." She wiggles the box in her hand.

Someone in a red vest speaks up before I can leave. "We don't. And personally, I'd prefer to get out of here on time today, so I can spend the evening with my family."

Chrissie nods in approval. "Right you are."

She surveys the crowd before speaking again. "Okay. We can do this one of two ways. One, I can buy this ornament and all of you lose. Or, I can pick one of you to get the ornament."

Shouts of "Pick me!" "Pick me!" ring through the store.

"Alright. Convince me of why you should be the one to get this ornament and it's yours." She points at the woman who was trying to steal the ornament. "You start."

The woman's face pales. "It's okay. Pick someone else. I can't afford it anyway." Her chin falls to her chest.

"We have a winner!" She glares at the crowd. "Are any of you going to give me a hard time as I leave here with her to buy this?"

Everyone shakes their head and Chrissie jumps down. She takes the woman's hand and marches to where I'm standing.

"Sorry, Bossy. I've got to check out with her. Do you want to pick out some ornaments and join us in the line?" She glances over at the check-out lanes. "I estimate we'll be in the line at least forty-five minutes." She addresses the woman, "What else do you need for Christmas? I'm Chrissie by the way."

The woman clears her throat. "I'm Jane, and I don't need anything else." Her stomach rumbles and she coughs to cover the sound.

"Okay. Check-out it is." Chrissie nods and they start toward the check-out. After a few steps, she glances over her shoulder and mouths to me *buy her everything*.

She didn't need to tell me. Of course, I'll buy the store out for Jane. I'm also going to buy every damn ornament I can find for my woman. And she wonders why I call her angel.

Chapter 34

What's another word for a Canadian spy? A double Eh 'gent.

I snuggle into Wally the next morning as I slowly wake up. When my mind switches on, I realize what day it is and knife up, accidentally hitting Wally in the forehead with my head in the process.

"Ouch." I pat my head to check for bleeding. Wally's head is freaking hard.

"Are you feeling violent after your adventure in mall shopping on Christmas Eve?" he asks as he rubs his forehead.

Yesterday's trip to the mall was too much fun. I kind of miss the adrenaline of fighting, and now I know I can head over to the mall whenever I need a fix.

"It's Christmas," I squeal before jumping out of bed. I grab his hand. "Come on. Present time."

Wally allows me to pull him out of bed. I lick my lips when I see him in all his naked glory standing next to the bed. No way is this man fifty-nine. It must be some trick.

"If you want to open presents, you need to stop looking at me like I'm a juicy steak."

"I—" Wait. What? "Open presents?"

When I snuck out of bed last night to place Wally's presents under our now decorated Christmas tree, there weren't any presents for me. I start rushing toward the living room, but Wally catches my hand and stops me.

"Clothes," he orders.

I give him a saucy wink. "You didn't seem to mind me naked in bed last night."

He spins me around and shoves me toward my walk-in closet. "Get some clothes on. I'll make breakfast."

By the time I dress, Wally is already putzing around in the kitchen. I sigh when I smell the coffee. I need a caffeine fix. After spending most of the afternoon at the mall, we still had to decorate the tree when we got home. It was late by the time we went to bed, and Wally didn't exactly let me sleep right away.

We got home? Since when do I consider this house home for Wally and me? I'm still undecided about him moving in, despite him thinking it's a done deal. It's not. Trust me.

When I enter the living room, my eyes catch on the Christmas tree. The area under the tree is now stuffed with presents. I gasp.

Wally rounds the kitchen island and walks over holding out a coffee cup for me. "You seriously didn't think I'd let you celebrate your first Christmas after all this time without spoiling you, did you?"

"But there weren't any presents under the tree when I put yours under there. And how did you manage to buy this many presents anyway?"

He cocks an eyebrow. "How did you manage to buy presents for me?"

I tip my non-existent hat at him. "Touché."

He hands me the coffee and kisses my forehead. "Presents or breakfast first."

"Are you seriously asking me?" Is he crazy? I may be inching toward fifty, but we are totally opening the presents first.

He chuckles and leads me to the living room. He gets me settled on the sofa before handing me the first box.

"Wait! You should go first."

"Too late." He nudges the box in my hand. "Open it."

I stare at the package a second before ripping the paper away. I tear the top of the box off to discover tissue paper. I slow down before I destroy whatever's inside. I remove the layers of tissue paper to find red material.

"A dress? You bought me a dress?"

I stand and place the dress in front of me. It has a sweetheart neckline, a wrapped ruched belt waist, and three-quarter sleeves. With its red color, it's the perfect Christmas dress.

"Do you like it?" For the first time since I met him, Wally seems uncertain.

"It's gorgeous."

He smiles. "I'm glad you like it." He hands me another box.

"Hey! I thought we were taking turns."

"This all goes together."

"Did you buy me naughty lingerie to wear under the dress?"

"You wouldn't get mad if I did?"

I wrinkle my nose. "Why would I get mad?"

He smirks. "I'll make a note of it." He nods to the box. "Now, open it."

I open the box to reveal a pair of pointed toe pumps in the same red color as the dress.

"Are we going somewhere I need to dress up for?"

He shrugs. "I thought you might like to get dressed up for Christmas."

He places another box on my lap. I glare at him, and he lifts his hands in surrender. "Last one for now."

I stare down at the box. The box is suspiciously the size of a jewelry box. "This is not more clothing."

"It's for the outfit."

"It's too much."

He nudges my knee. "How do you know? You haven't opened it yet."

I lift the top of the box and gasp at the contents – a white gold chain with a ruby drop pendant and matching ruby earrings.

"Do you like it?"

Before I have a chance to answer, Wally removes the necklace from the box and secures it around my neck.

"The red is gorgeous against your pale skin. And it matches your dress."

I play with the pendant. "You've got good taste, Bossy."

"I have the best taste. I chose you, didn't I?" He kisses my neck, and I sigh. "I love you, Angel."

I take a deep breath and force the words out of my mouth. "I love you, too, but you're still bossy."

He chuckles before dropping down to sit next to me. "Your turn."

I clap and jump to my feet. "Finally."

I find one of the presents for him and place it in his lap. I sit back on my knees and bite my lip while he opens it.

"I hope you like it."

"It's my first Christmas gift from you. I'll love it."

He dawdles as he removes the gift wrap. I grunt, and he winks at me. Annoying man. He's torturing me on purpose. Typical.

"Wow," he says when he finally opens the box.

"Do you like it?"

I bought him a pair of noise cancelling earphones with Bluetooth. "They're for noise protection while you're doing your woodworking, but you can also listen to music or a podcast or talk to someone on the phone while you're wearing them."

He palms my neck and squeezes. "I love them. I can't wait to try them out."

"Yeah!"

I return to the tree and grab a bigger box. "I can return it if you already have it," I say as I set it on his lap.

He growls. "I'm not returning a gift from you – ever."

"Just wait."

This time he doesn't torture me as he opens his gift. His eyes widen when he reads the box. "A SwitchDriver."

"Do you already have one? The guy at the store said this is the perfect addition to any woodworker's workshop. It's a favorite at their store. You can drill holes and drive screws without carrying two drills or switching out the bit."

He chuckles at me, and I switch off my mouth to shrug.

"I don't have one. This is going to come in handy when I set up my woodworking shop in the shed."

I'm too happy to start an argument about him building a shed in my yard again. I whip around and crawl to the tree to find another present. When I pull out another box, something falls. I shove the big box out of the way to discover a small one. I snag it and crawl out from under the tree.

"What's—"

My words die in my throat when I notice Wally is now down on one knee. My eyes widen and I shake my head. "No. No. No. No. Too fast."

Wally snatches the box from me and flips it open. When I see the contents, my heartbeat quickens until I have to clutch my chest to stop my heart from beating right out of my body.

"Angel, I know giving an engagement ring for a Christmas present is cliché, but I don't give a crap."

"Wow. When you said you weren't waiting to get what you want, you weren't kidding. Talk about full steam ahead."

He clutches my hand. "Let's get married."

My eyebrows fly off my forehead. "That's it? No heartfelt speech? No romantic proposal?"

He smirks. "Angel, I know you don't give a shit about romance and speeches. You want the truth." I nod. He's not lying. Romance is for the young.

"How about this? I love you. You love me. I'm moving in. Let's make it official."

I cross my arms over my chest. "We haven't agreed to you moving in yet."

"Baby, you noticed my clothes in your drawers and you didn't kick me out."

I huff. "Because I needed time to think about it."

"If you needed time, you would have kicked me out and told me to come back when you were good and ready."

I glare at him, but my glare has no effect on this man. He stays kneeling, staring up at me, his eyes full of hope and happiness.

"Please, I want to replace your sad Christmas memories with good ones."

Ugh! How does he know the correct thing to say all the time? "Fine. Let's get married. But I want a long engagement."

"Whatever you want, Angel. Whatever you want." Why don't I believe him?

Chapter 35

A spy was killed in his tea. He paid a steep price
for what he knew.

"You're looking mighty sexy, Mr. Bossy." Wally's wearing a three-piece suit with a tie the exact color of the dress I'm wearing.

He threads his fingers through my hair. "I ain't got nothing on you, Mrs. Soon-to-be-Bossy."

At his words, I glance down at the pear-shaped diamond ring on my finger. I blink, but when I open my eyes, the ring is still there.

Wally uses his hold on my hair to lift my face. "It's real. We're real. And I'm never going to let you go."

"Stalker much?"

I can feel the smile on his face when he kisses my forehead before releasing my hair and stepping back. "We need to get going or we'll be late."

I wag a finger at him. "Don't be mad at me. You're the one who climbed into the shower with me. I told you if my hair got wet, we were going to be late."

"It was worth it."

Yeah, it was.

We climb into his truck and drive to McGraw's Pub where the entire gang celebrates Christmas together. Wally keeps a steadying hand on my back as we navigate over the slippery parking lot to the front door. Right before he opens the door, he pauses and turns to me.

"Don't be mad."

Before I have a chance to ask him what the hell he's talking about, he opens the door and ushers me inside. I survey the room. What's going on? Instead of a big table in the middle of the room to accommodate the entire group of us eating a Christmas meal, chairs are set up in rows before a small stage.

"What's happening?"

People pour out of the hallway into the bar area. "Surprise!"

"Welcome to your wedding," Wally says.

"Wait! What? I thought this was Faith and Max's wedding. Wally and Chrissie are getting married?" Suzie sighs. "Welp. I lost that bet."

Lenny rubs his hands together. "I didn't. Pay up suckers."

"Nope. How do we know you didn't have inside information? Someone had to set this up." Hailey motions to the chairs and stage.

"I set it up this morning, baby girl," Max says. "After Wally called to tell me it's his wedding day."

"He didn't tell me!" I shout. "He literally proposed this morning. I specifically said yes with the condition we would have a long engagement." I check my watch. "Three hours and twenty minutes is not a long time by anyone's measure."

"I told you I wasn't waiting," Wally grumbles.

I spin around and advance on him. "Guess what? I get a say in this, too. It's a relationship. You can't have a relationship with one person. And I'm not ready." I stomp my foot.

"She's gonna blow!" Suzie shouts.

"Not helping," Faith mutters before nabbing my hand and leading me to the back hallway. Hailey, Phoebe, Suzie, Valerie, and Mary Ann follow us.

"Are we having a party in the restroom?" Suzie asks before shouting behind her. "Send in some champagne!"

"I think we better stick to tequila," Hailey mumbles under her breath.

Faith ushers me into Max's office and pushes me down on the sofa. "Why are you stalling?"

"Yeah," Valerie adds. "I'd marry Wally in a heartbeat."

Faith rolls her eyes. "Liar. You're terrified of getting married."

"And you're in love with Barney," Suzie adds.

"Why are you terrified of marriage?" I ask.

Hailey wags her finger in my face. "Oh no, you don't. No stalling. We'll deal with Valerie and her problems later."

"Hey! I don't have any problems." I may not know Valerie well, but she's obviously lying.

"Can I sit down next to you?" Phoebe asks before collapsing next to me. "How is it Suzie is handling pregnancy better than me? She's a munchkin."

"A mighty munchkin!" Suzie places on fist on her hip and throws her other fist in the air.

"Mighty mouse is more like," Phoebe grumbles.

Faith claps her hands. "Children. Can we focus on the problem at hand, please?"

There's a knock on the door before Ollie peeks his head in. "I have champagne."

Faith purses her lips. "The door was locked."

Ollie smirks up at his mom. "Pops taught me how to pick a lock."

Hailey high-fives him. "Right on, brother."

Faith tries a different tactic. "We're going to talk about girl stuff."

He feigns gagging before handing a bottle of champagne to Mary Ann. "Pops says the glasses are in the cabinet," he says before disappearing.

Mary Ann finds the glasses and pops the champagne bottle before pouring glasses for the five non-pregnant women. "I need to convince Sid to allow me to come with him to the pub more often. It's always a good time."

"Does he not allow you to come here?"

She waves a hand at me. "Don't worry. He doesn't order me around. I wouldn't put up with it."

"Oh, your ring is gorgeous, Chrissie." Phoebe grabs my hand and studies my diamond. "And those earrings and necklace. Wally has good taste."

"You didn't help him?" I was certain he had her help him pick everything out. "Did you help with the dress?"

"Nope. I would have helped, but he didn't ask. He's a dark horse."

Hailey snorts. "Duh. Super-secret soldier, remember?"

Suzie plops down in a chair across from us and sets her feet on the coffee table. She rubs her belly as she asks, "What can you tell us about the super-secret soldier, Chrissie?"

I give her the look. She covers her face with her hands. "Mom, she's giving me the look."

"Your mom isn't here," I point out.

She points to Faith. "She's our substitute mom."

Faith huffs. "Are you serious? I'm not even the oldest person in the room."

"But you are the only mom."

There's a knock on the door before Wally asks, "Can I speak to my bride?"

"There's no one in here who answers to that description," I shout. The nerve of the man!

"I need a minute," Faith shouts before Wally can respond.

She waits until we hear his footsteps fade away before speaking, "Do you love Wally?"

Geez. What is it with everyone asking me if I love Wally lately? "Yes." I sound like a petulant teenager.

"Do you want to marry him?"

"Isn't it too soon?" I look to Phoebe. "It's too soon, isn't it?"

She shrugs. "Don't ask me. I married my kidnapper."

I glance around the room for support.

Suzie lifts her hands in front of her. "Don't look at me. Grayson sprung a Vegas wedding on me without telling me first."

Faith kneels in front of me and grasps my hands. "It's your choice. If you aren't prepared to marry Wally today, I'll march out there and tell him so while these women sneak you out the back door."

This sounds like a good plan to me.

"I wish someone had offered me a getaway at my first marriage," she confesses.

"Amen!" Valerie shouts.

"I knew something was wrong, but everything was arranged, and I felt like I couldn't get off the rollercoaster."

Valerie raises her hand. "I did try to shove her off."

"She did, but I didn't listen." Faith clears her throat. "Do you feel like it's not right?" When I don't answer right away, she squeezes my hands. "Well?"

"No," I finally admit. "It's almost too perfect. Have you met Wally? He's like the perfect man. He does the sweetest things for me. He bought me this whole outfit. He decorated my house for Christmas because he knew I hadn't celebrated since my parents died. He makes me feel special."

"I think you answered your own question."

"But what if it doesn't last? What if he becomes someone I don't recognize?"

I wish I could tell them about Flynn Price and what he did to me – how he turned traitor while ruining my reputation and faith in mankind – but there's basically no one I can talk to about what happened. Stupid top-secret clearance bullshit.

Hailey joins Faith. "We've all got our pasts. Suzie here nearly let her past ruin her relationship with Grayson."

Suzie nods. "It's true."

"And I nearly didn't give Aiden a chance despite loving him for over a decade. The question is – are you going to let your past ruin your future? Or are you going to pick up your lady balls and marry the man you love?" She raises her voice. "The man we all know is eavesdropping right now."

"Wally's pacing the bar like a caged animal. I'm not listening. I'm only here to ensure Chrissie doesn't escape," Lenny shouts through the door.

Hailey stands and holds out her hand. "I didn't figure you for a chicken."

"Bwak bwak," Suzie clucks like a chicken.

I bite my lip as I think about what she said. I know she's right. I am letting my past dictate my actions right now. Flynn fucking Price tried his damndest to ruin my life. Well, you know what? I'm not going to let him.

I stand. "Fine. Let's do this!"

Chapter 36

Your spy name is your last name, followed by a
brief pause, and then your first name and new
last name.

HAILEY OPENS THE DOOR to find Pops standing there waiting for us. He clears his throat. "Um, if it's alright with you, I'd like to accompany you down the aisle. I know I'm not old enough to be your father, and I know I could never replace your father, but I'm here and," his eyes sparkle, "I have a bit of experience in giving away the bride."

I glance over at Hailey and cock my eyebrow. I need to know she doesn't have a problem with me stealing her dad for a few minutes.

She smiles. "I'm happy to share my father with everyone. After all, he's got a lot of love to share."

"He certainly does," Faith chimes in.

Hailey rises up on her tiptoes to kiss her father's cheek before sauntering off behind the group of women making their way to the main area of the bar.

Max holds out his elbow. "You ready, Chrissie?"

I snort. "Are you kidding? I only admitted I loved Wally a few nights ago, got engaged this morning, and now I'm getting married. I'm surprised my head isn't literally spinning in circles like we're in some horror movie."

He turns to me and cups my chin. "If you're not ready, say the word and I'll have you out the back door and on your way to some exotic destination before Wally realizes what happened."

I tilt my head and scrunch my nose. "What exotic destination?"

He chuckles and drops his hands. "You're ready."

He holds out his elbow again and this time I thread my arm through his. "Wally's a good guy. He will cherish you and protect you and love you until his dying breath."

"My head knows this. My heart is having trouble believing he won't change."

He squeezes my hand. "Considering what happened to you, it's amazing you're such a sweet and loving person. I'm proud of you."

Tears well in my eyes, and I come to a halt to glare up at him. "If you make me cry and ruin my make-up before I get married, I will hurt you. I know where you live."

He grins before kissing my cheek. "Sorry, darling."

The music starts up and when the first notes of *All I Want for Christmas is You* play, I burst out laughing. Damn Wally, and his ability to know the perfect thing to say or do to get him out of the doghouse. This does not bode well for our future. Not for my future at least.

We enter the bar, and everyone stands before craning their necks around to watch as Max and I walk down the aisle. I ignore everyone to find Wally. He's standing on the stage, his hand worrying his neck as he paces up and down. When his eyes meet mine, he freezes, and a smile lights up his face.

The door slams open, and I duck before spinning around with my weapon raised.

"Sorry, I'm late," Lexi says as she walks to me. "But someone," she glares at Wally, "didn't give me much notice."

I snort. "Yeah, well, I didn't have much notice myself."

She throws her arms around me. "I'm so happy for you."

I feel tears well in my eyes and do the logical thing. I sneer at her. "Don't make me cry."

She lifts her arms and retreats. "Sorry. Not sorry." She winks. "Now, go get married."

She saunters off to find a seat, and I notice Lenny's gaze never leaves hers as she sits across from the aisle in front of him. Huh. I thought Lenny was into men.

The music starts up again and I return the weapon to the holster under my dress before Max and I begin marching down the makeshift aisle again. I keep my eyes focused on Wally. I can tell by the way his body rocks forward that he can barely stand still and wait for me. The idea this man – the eternal bachelor – can't wait for me to walk down the aisle to him causes my heart to settle. Flynn Price was never excited to see me to the point he could barely stand still.

And that's the last time I compare Flynn to Wally. It's unfair to Wally, and I am done with my past. D-O-N-E. Done. I take a deep breath, shove all the memories of Flynn and what happened into a box in my mind before locking the box and shoving it into the furthest corner of my mind.

"Damn it," Barney swears and jars me out of my head. "I was positive Wally would pull an Aiden and dash down the aisle to grab Chrissie from Pops' arms."

Lenny tuts. "He's waited fifty-nine years to find his bride. Of course, he wasn't going to run down the aisle and ruin the moment. You owe me twenty."

I glance over at Wally's brothers and just for fun give them my look. Barney yelps and turns away, but Lenny and Sid smirk at me while Mary Ann gives me a thumbs-up.

We continue a few paces and stop in front of Wally and the preacher. How the heck did Wally get a preacher here on Christmas day? It's probably better not to ask.

"Who gives this woman to be married to this man?" the preacher asks.

I open my mouth to tell them no one, I give my darn self, but everyone in the room shouts, "We do!"

I spin around to survey the group. Everyone is smiling wide. Hailey winks at me, Lexi gives me a thumbs-up, and Faith mouths *You got this!* I do got this. With my friends at my back, I can do anything. And to think, I didn't know most of these crazy people three months ago. I didn't know what I was missing.

Max kisses my hair before growling at Wally, "Take care of her."

"Always, brother. Always," he answers Max, but he's looking at me as he says the words.

Max steps back and I join Wally on the stage. He takes my hands before kissing my forehead. "Thank you, Angel."

What is he thanking me for? "I didn't do anything."

"You're here. It's all that matters."

My tummy warms, and I elbow him. "Don't make me cry. As long as we're doing this thing, I want pictures."

"I got you covered," Hailey shouts and holds up her camera.

The preacher clears his throat. "Can we begin?"

"Sorry. Go ahead."

"Family and friends, thank you all for coming today to share in this wonderful occasion. Today, we are here together to unite Walter Nelson and Christina Lindberg in marriage."

I snort. "Walter."

"Shush, you."

"Walter, I understand you have written your own vows."

Uh oh. I'm not prepared. I didn't write vows. Before I can go into full blown panic mode, Wally speaks.

"I know you think I'm pushy."

"Bossy," I correct him.

He grins. "I know you think I'm bossy." He pauses to wait for me to interrupt again, but I only nod in agreement. "But I wanted to replace your sad memories of Christmas with good ones, and I wasn't willing to wait a year to make it happen."

I feel my lower lip tremble, so I do the adult thing. I slap his chest. "Stop being sweet!"

"Get used to it, Angel, because after today you are mine. I vow to take care of you, to spoil you, to protect you, and to love you until the last breath leaves my body. I promise I will never take your love and loyalty for granted and I will never betray you."

"Christina, do you have vows prepared?"

"I'll wing it." I squeeze Wally's hands before opening my mouth and letting it all flow out, "I love you Walter Nelson, and I will love you until the end of time. I promise to put up with your bossiness as much as I can. And when it gets to be too much, I'll let you sleep in the shed instead of kicking your royal bossiness out. I promise to stand by your side when times are good. And, when times are bad, I'll stand behind you to keep you standing."

Wally growls. "You will not support me. It's my job to support you."

"Too bad. These are my vows. You did your vows. It's my turn now."

His growl switches off, and I continue, "And when you get old and decrepit before me, since you're already an old man, I'll take care of and let you whine about all your aches and pains."

"I'll show you aches and pains," he grumbles.

"I think that covers it all," I tell the preacher.

He shakes his head, but the corners of his lips are turned up in amusement. "May I have the rings, please?"

Oh no. We don't have rings. Max stands and places two wedding bands in Wally's hand.

"How?" I ask, but then throw up a hand to stop his answer. "Never mind. I should know better than to ask."

"Walter, place the ring on your bride's finger."

I slip off my engagement ring and hold out my left hand.

"Repeat after me. With this ring, I thee wed and pledge you my love now and forever."

Wally places a white gold ring on my finger. "With this ring, I thee wed and pledge you my love now and forever." He lifts up my hand and kisses my fingers. "I love you, Angel."

I motion for him to hurry up and hand me his ring. I want Wally to wear my ring. He chuckles as he places it in my palm. I stick my tongue out at him before placing the ring on his finger. "With this ring, I thee wed and pledge you my love now and forever."

"By the authority vested in me by the State of Wisconsin, I now pronounce you husband and wife. You may kiss your bride."

Wally wraps his arm around my waist and pulls me near. "I love you, Angel."

As soon as his lips meet mine, hoots and hollers erupt in the room. I think I even hear someone shout Yee-haw. This crazy group. Gotta love them.

Wally spins me around and takes my hand before leading me to the edge of the stage. "You ready?"

"For everything," I say, and we jump off.

We're bombarded by well wishes from our friends the moment we land. Except for one brother. Barney is sneaking off toward the hallway leading to the restrooms. The same hallway Valerie is standing at the mouth of.

"This is gonna be fun," I murmur while watching Barney rush after Valerie.

"It sure is," Wally says, but he isn't looking at Barney and Valerie, he's looking at me. "Gotcha, Angel."

D. E. Haggerty
Love and Laughter in Every Chapter

About the Author

D.E. Haggerty is an American who has spent the majority of her adult life abroad. She has lived in Istanbul, various places throughout Germany, and currently finds herself in The Hague. She has been a military policewoman, a lawyer, a B&B owner/operator and now a writer.